THE CARNELIAN MOON

Novels by John Michael Greer

Ariel Moravec Occult Mysteries
The Witch of Criswell
The Book of Haatan

The Weird of Hali
I – Innsmouth
II – Kingsport
III – Chorazin
IV – Dreamlands
V – Providence
VI – Red Hook
VII – Arkham

Others
The Fires of Shalsha
Star's Reach
Twilight's Last Gleaming
Retrotopia
The Shoggoth Concerto
The Nyogtha Variations
A Voyage to Hyperborea
The Seal of Yueh Lao
Journey Star

THE CARNELIAN MOON

An Ariel Moravec Occult Mystery

John Michael Greer

First published in 2024 by
Sphinx Books
London

Copyright © 2024 by John Michael Greer

The right of John Michael Greer to be identified as the author of this work has been asserted in accordance with §§ 77 and 78 of the Copyright Design and Patents Act 1988.

All rights reserved. No part of this publication may be reproduced, stored in a retrieval system, or transmitted, in any form or by any means, electronic, mechanical, photocopying, recording, or otherwise, without the prior written permission of the publisher.

British Library Cataloguing in Publication Data

A C.I.P. for this book is available from the British Library

ISBN-13: 978-1-91595-224-0

Typeset by Medlar Publishing Solutions Pvt Ltd, India

www.aeonbooks.co.uk/sphinx

Chapter 1

WHEN THE WOLFBANE BLOOMS

The lights came up in the theater, bleaching out the last of the credits on the screen. Ariel Moravec blinked and shook herself. The frightful fate suffered by Lon Chaney Jr. in the final scene of *The Wolf Man* dissolved, replaced all at once by the more prosaic if less monochrome realities of a cramped and slightly dilapidated movie house starting its second century. Wine-colored curtains to either side lurched inward and attempted, not quite successfully, to cover the screen. Most of the audience lurched, too, and filed out awkwardly into the narrow aisles.

"Time to go," said Danny Jackson, two seats away from Ariel, and started to get up.

"Nope," said his sister Cassie, who sat between them. "You'll just have to stand longer."

"Oh, come on—"

"Nope," she repeated. "You want to sit close to the screen, you get to wait." He glared at her but sat back down. Past him, his older brother Orion chuckled but said nothing.

The Jacksons had a black father and a Korean mother, and it showed: medium brown skin, black hair somewhere between straight and wavy, broad cheekbones, and the little fold on the corner of the eyelids announcing East Asian ancestry. No two of them had the same build, though. Cassie, eighteen, was short and stocky; Orion, sixteen, was long and lean, and stood head and shoulders taller than his sister. Danny, fourteen, still had the coltish look of his age but his shoulders were bulking out almost as fast as he was putting on height. Ariel was the odd one out in the party, a familiar condition for her: thin and a little gawky, pale skin already shedding its light summer tan, straight black hair cut to shoulder length, large brown eyes dominating a small nose and chin.

Two or three minutes passed and the press at the exits began to thin. Ariel glanced at Cassie, who nodded, and the two of them stood up together and filed out into the aisle, followed by the boys. Once the last of the crowd cleared, the aisle spilled them out into a cramped lobby redolent with the smell of buttered popcorn. The lobby, doors gaping open, carried out the same operation and launched them onto a cracked and stained sidewalk. Overhead, yellow neon letters spelled out APOLLO THEATER. Below that, the brightly lit marquee had its own message:

LON CHANEY JR. IN
THE WOLF MAN
OWOOO

"So what do you think?" Orion asked Ariel as the four of them moved with the crowd along the sidewalk.

"That was the bee's knees," Ariel said. The two boys gave her baffled looks. Cassie, who'd had two months to get used to Ariel's habits, choked back a laugh and told her, "You're going to have to translate that."

"Really great," Ariel said, reddening.

"They used to say that back in the nineteen-twenties, right?" said Orion.

"Yeah." Ariel shrugged. "I like to read books from back then, and saying 'dank' and 'lit' and things like that always seemed kind of dumb to me." Before any of them could argue: "Does the Apollo always run old movies?"

"These days? Yeah," said Orion. "When I was a kid, about the time we moved up here, they still ran new stuff sometimes, but there was some kind of contract problem or something. There was all kinds of stuff about it in the news. So they started running old black and white movies instead, like this one, and folks ate it up."

"You sure did," Cassie said. To Ariel: "One time he went every night for a week."

Orion grinned. "You better believe I did. They ran a double bill all week, *Stormy Weather* and *Cabin in the Sky*. You know those?"

Ariel shook her head, but she could guess the reason easily enough from what she'd already learned of his interests. "Jazz films?"

Orion nodded enthusiastically. "Oh, yeah. Lena Horne starred in both of 'em, Cab Calloway and Bojangles Robinson were in one, and Ethel Waters and Louis Armstrong were in the other. I was in *heaven*."

Danny made a rude noise down in his throat. "You'd have been someplace a lot hotter if Cassie and me didn't cover for you. Mom would have just about killed you if she found out."

"I got my homework done," Orion protested.

"By flashlight," said Danny. "You were up 'til, what? Two in the morning?"

A street corner with crosswalks gave the crowd a chance to disperse. Ariel and the Jacksons waited for the light to change, crossed with a stream of others, kept going.

"Look!" said Cassie, pointing back behind them into the gathering darkness of the eastern sky. There, up above the rooftops, a full moon shone down.

"Like the rhyme in the movie," Danny said. "How did that go?"

"Even a man who is pure in heart and says his prayers by night—" Orion chanted. When he faltered, trying to remember the next words, Cassie took over: "May become a wolf when the wolfbane blooms and the autumn moon is bright." Like her brothers, she pronounced the animal's name "woof."

Danny threw back his head and attempted a wolf howl: "Owooo!" It wasn't very convincing, Ariel thought, and stifled a grin.

Orion wasn't so polite. "Come on," he said. "That sounds like a werepoodle."

"The autumn moon's not bright enough," said Cassie.

"Someone's not bright enough," Orion said in response. Danny tried to cuff him. Orion, laughing, fended off the blow.

"Okay, Mister Big Mouth," said Danny, "let's see you do it."

Orion turned to Cassie. "Help me, okay?" The two of them raised their faces and howled, or tried to. The joint effort wasn't much better than Danny's, and it didn't help that Cassie started laughing partway through and finished her share of the howl with a kind of half-syncopated gasp.

"Oh man," said Danny, laughing too. "A werepoodle with hiccups." That made Cassie laugh even harder.

"You got to help us, Ariel," Orion said then. "Every real wolf in America's got to be giving us the side-eye right about now."

"Well—"

"Come on," said Cassie. "Let's hear it."

"Okay." Ariel drew in a deep breath, brought to mind everything she knew about the songs of her favorite animal, and howled. It started out long and low, and rose bit by bit to a shuddering peak, then fell away into silence. Long before she'd finished, all three Jacksons were staring at her, and so were passersby on both sides of the street.

"You learned that from a wolf," said Danny.

"Yeah, kind of," said Ariel. They turned a corner, started uphill on Lyon Avenue. "My folks used to send me to camp every summer. One time it was out west, and there were wolves in the hills close by. I used to go outside at night to get away from the other girls, and just listen to the wolves howling. That was the one good thing about that whole summer."

"Come on," said Danny. "Out in the woods with wolves and everything? What's not great about that?"

"Sure, if the wolves aren't chewing on you," said Cassie.

"Or the other kids," Ariel said. "It was the kind of place where some of the girls were from families that helped get the camp started, and as far as the staff was concerned they could do no wrong. They knew it, too, and they bullied everyone else."

"You should have kicked their—" Danny growled. Cassie shot a hard look at him, and he let the sentence drop unfinished.

"That's kind of hard when it's nine or ten on one," Ariel pointed out.

Danny considered that, shrugged. "I suppose. I never got to go to summer camp."

Cassie sent another look his way, harder. "That's not true at all! You went to day camp like the rest of us."

"What's day camp?" Ariel asked, puzzled.

"The parks department here does it every summer," said Cassie. "And they have it across the water, too—that's where I went, when we still lived in South." Ariel knew already that this was shorthand for South Adocentyn, the down-at-heels suburb across Coopers Bay. "Nine in the morning to five in the afternoon six days a week, games and crafts and nature walks and museums and all kinds of other fun stuff. They didn't have that in Summerfield?"

"I wish," Ariel said, meaning it. "All the good parts of camp, and then you get to go home to your own room and shut the door and not have to deal with anybody."

"Yeah, but there aren't any wolves around," said Danny.

"You keep that up," Cassie told him, "and something that's not a wolf is going to bite your butt good and hard." He laughed, but let the subject drop.

By that point they had left behind commercial buildings and were passing three- and four-story houses with clapboard sides. A little further and they crossed March Street. "You gonna be okay the rest of the way?" Danny asked Ariel.

"Yeah, I'll be fine. It's just three blocks."

"Okay, see you," he said, and Cassie: "See you Monday." Orion grinned and mimed lifting a nonexistent hat. The three of them headed east on March Street.

Ariel kept going up Lyon Avenue. Around her, night deepened and the stars glittered in a clear sky. Scraps of the movie she'd watched tumbled around in her mind along with bits of conversation from before and after. Cassie's words about day camp, in particular, stirred up stray thoughts. Growing up in suburban Summerfield, she'd thought of summer camp as something everyone did. That Cassie and her brothers hadn't shared the experience left her feeling unsettled, as though some minor law of nature had just been turned on its head. After a moment, she mocked herself for feeling that way, but the feeling still lingered.

The last block of Lyon Avenue, where the great oaks of Culpeper Park loomed up ahead against the stars, came sooner than she expected. To one side was the big Victorian house her grandfather owned. No light showed in the windows: no surprises there. She let herself in and locked the door behind her. Light spilling in windows from the streetlamp outside let her see well enough to hang her coat on the big coat tree in the entry.

She went on into the parlor and turned on one of the lamps by the sofa. Yellow light spilled over tall bookshelves full of antique books of magic, curious diagrams in ornate frames, a grandfather clock with extra dials that tracked the moon and the planets, and a little wooden crocodile, perched atop one bookshelf, who gazed down with a toothy smile. Ariel smiled back at it and headed for the kitchen.

There she checked for phone messages and found none, then got out a pan and fixed a couple of burritos with fillings from bowls in the fridge. She'd found the note from her grandfather on the kitchen table earlier that day: *Ariel—at Heydonian until late. You're on your own for dinner.* No surprises there, either, for he was on the board of trustees of the Heydonian Institution, Adocentyn's sprawling library and museum of magic. Very long workdays came with that position now and then.

The rest of the evening went past unremarkably. She spent much of it picking her way through a French book on magic her grandfather had instructed her to read, an ornate tome by a nineteenth-century writer who used the pen name Papus. Well before midnight, she made sure the house was properly locked up and went upstairs to her bedroom.

A wolf waited for her on the bed, but it wasn't the kind that might startle her with a sudden howl or bite. She'd gotten it on her twelfth birthday at a zoo's gift shop: a stuffed plush timber wolf fully three feet long, with a pink tongue lolling between felt teeth. Its name was Nicodemus, and the fact that she still slept curled up around it at the age of eighteen was the guiltiest of her few guilty secrets.

She ruffled the fur on the wolf's shoulders and started getting ready for bed, then stopped and went over to her desk. That night and every night, and every morning for that matter, she had work to do.

Just two months before, she'd helped her grandfather unravel an intricate puzzle in which a stolen book, a series of unsolved burglaries, and a centuries-old legend of pirate treasure all played a role. After that experience, she'd taken up serious training in the ancient art of magic. Her grandfather had warned her then that some of the practices would be duller than anything else she'd ever done. She'd known better than to think he was joking, but his warning had turned out even more on target than she imagined. Only the stubborn streak that had gotten her through a difficult childhood kept her at it after two months of unrelieved twice-daily boredom.

The practice itself was simple enough. She turned on the little lamp on the desk and turned off the overhead light, leaving most of the bedroom in shadow and transforming the roses on the wallpaper into dim cryptic shapes. Her crystal ball—a gift from her grandfather, a fine two-inch sphere of clear quartz crystal—came out of its velvet pouch in one of her desk drawers; its place was on a little metal stand, which rested on a square of black velvet.

Once the preparations were finished, Ariel sat in her chair facing the ball and made a gesture with both hands, like drawing the two sides of a curtain apart—the opening gesture, her grandfather called it. Then she tried to relax every muscle she could without falling out of the chair. After that, she did a simple breathing exercise for five minutes exactly, keeping time by the clock on her desk, and turned her gaze to the center of the crystal ball for another five minutes, holding her mind as clear as she could and waiting for images to appear.

Simple, her grandfather had warned her, was not the same as easy. In the two months she'd been doing the practice, she'd found out just how true that was. Most times nothing happened at all. Now and again, a faint clouding like mist seemed to appear in the middle of the crystal: a good sign, Dr. Moravec told her, an indication that she was beginning to perceive the astral light that flowed through all things. So far, though, the mist hadn't dissolved to show her an image of something else. That was the next step, so the books said, but it might take months or even years of daily practice before that happened reliably.

It didn't help that scraps of thought and memory kept surfacing in her mind, distracting her from the crystal. At first, as she tried to keep her attention focused, images from *The Wolf Man* kept surfacing, mostly Lon Chaney Jr. in all the furry glory given him by the makeup artist. Maria Ouspenskaya, who'd played a Romani fortune-teller, also put in a few appearances. Ariel managed to chase those images off, but bits of the conversation she'd had with Cassie and her brothers followed, and then a cascade of wretched memories from the summer camp in Colorado where she'd listened to the wolves at night.

It took repeated efforts to pull her attention away from those and focus on the crystal again, but that action simply set off another cascade of thoughts. Those tumbled around the first time she'd tried to see visions in a crystal, when she'd helped her grandfather perform a spell from an old volume of magic called *The Book of Haatan*. That time she hadn't had to struggle at all. His voice, chanting words in Latin and strange names of power, had swept aside wandering thoughts and put her into contact with the spirit Haatan, who guarded and revealed treasures. Before the end of the following day she'd helped uncover a pirate treasure worth just over a million dollars.

That treasure wasn't hers to spend. That didn't trouble her, since the couple who'd gotten it needed it much more than she did, and they'd donated a good share of it to charity, too. She was beginning to daydream about maybe someday finding a treasure of her own when she caught herself, reddened, and forced her attention back to the crystal. The clock showed a minute still to go. She gritted her teeth, made herself relax again and wait out the last of the practice session.

A few moments passed, and then a faint blurred presence like haze in summer showed in the heart of the crystal. Ariel blinked, wondering if she was getting too tired to focus, but the haze remained.

Then, slowly, the haze thickened and a gray shape seemed to move through it. It took Ariel a moment to recognize the shape, because it never quite emerged from the haze, but then it turned yellow eyes toward her and she recognized it: a wolf, a big gray timber wolf. She could see it only for an instant, and then it faded back into the haze, which vanished in its turn.

A sidelong glance at the clock told her that she'd finished the five-minute session. She looked at the crystal for a few moments longer anyway, in case the wolf came back, and then made another simple gesture with both hands, drawing the imaginary curtain shut: the closing gesture. Half-formed habits got the crystal ball back in its velvet bag, and the bag, stand, and cloth into the desk drawer where they spent their off hours. Then she got a clothbound blank book and a pen out of the same drawer. Every practice, her grandfather had told her, had to be written down in a practice journal: what she'd done, what difficulties she'd had, and what if anything she'd seen in the crystal.

She had no difficulty noting the time of the practice and summing up the intrusive thoughts she'd wrestled with. The wolf was another matter, and she sat there with the cap of the pen pressed against one corner of her mouth, trying to decide if it was a scrap of imagery from the movie or something more. There were no real wolves in *The Wolf Man*, she recalled, but she noted it down as a distraction, put journal and pen away, and finished getting ready for bed.

As she settled under the covers with Nicodemus's synthetic fur pressed against one side of her face, Lon Chaney Jr.'s face in werewolf makeup surfaced in her mind's eye again. It's just a movie, she told herself groggily. People can't actually turn into wolves.

Can they?

Sleep drowned her thoughts before they went any further.

Chapter 2

A GIFT TO SORANUS

Werewolves were far from Ariel's mind when she woke the next morning. The weather outside was gray and cold, and rain pattered against the window close to her bed. She gave the world outside a bleary look, turned away from it, pulled the covers close around her and tried to get back to sleep.

The attempt didn't accomplish much. After a few minutes, she untangled herself from Nicodemus and crawled out of bed. A hot shower helped chase off the chill of the morning, and so did comfortable jeans and a warm sweater in a shade of forest green she liked. The thought of a big cup of hot coffee to finish the process made her start toward the door of her room, but she caught herself, turned around and made herself walk over to the desk for her morning practice.

The wolf didn't appear in the crystal that morning. Neither did anything else, barring a few faint patches of mist that vanished as soon as she noticed them. An itch that showed up on the tip of her nose the moment she started concentrating on the crystal didn't help matters any. Still, she gave the practice session its share of her morning. Once that was done she wrote down the details in her practice journal, put everything away, scooped up a battered hardback book titled Gregg Shorthand from the far corner of her desk, and headed downstairs.

The coffee maker was clearing its throat loudly when she got to the bottom of the stairs, as though it meant to draw her attention to something. Once she'd dropped the book on the sofa in the parlor, she took the hint and went into the kitchen. Her grandfather had gotten there already, though he wasn't after the coffee. He stood by the phone, a tall gaunt figure in a black suit, silver-haired and silver-bearded. The handset was pressed against one side of his face as he wrote something down on a notepad. Ariel knew better than to distract him. She got two slices of bread into the toaster, poured herself a cup of coffee, fixed it with cream and sugar, went back out to the parlor and settled comfortably on the couch to wait for her toast.

Dr. Moravec was still on the phone when the toast popped up, though he'd finished writing and was answering the person on the other end with brief phrases and the occasional monosyllable. Ariel flopped the toast on a plate, scraped butter and marmalade on it, and took it back out to the parlor, where she curled up on the sofa again and opened the book she'd brought downstairs. Scrying in a crystal wasn't the only obscure practice from the past she'd taken up: the loops and squiggles of shorthand filled the pages in front of her. She picked her way through the lesson, and then got a pen and a spiral-bound notebook from the end table and started copying the sentences one at a time into it.

That and the toast occupied the time while her grandfather finished the phone call and then made his own invariable breakfast: two poached eggs on toast, kippers, and coffee. He settled in his usual armchair across the parlor from the sofa, and had downed a good third of his coffee before he spoke to her. "Good morning, Ariel."

"Good morning. Was the call anything I should know about?"

"Yes, as it happens. A case."

She set her coffee cup down. "I'm all ears."

He used the edge of his spoon to cut into one of the poached eggs before going on. "The call was from Dr. Terry O'Shaughnessy from the Heydonian, the director of research, with the latest word on the Harshaw estate," he said.

Ariel winced. She'd seen Clarence Harshaw only a few times, but the last of those was burnt into her memory: a corpse sprawled on the sidewalk four stories below a shattered window, the victim of his own magical curse.

"I know," said Dr. Moravec.

She glanced up at him, sent an uncertain smile his way.

"Everything Harshaw owned is being sold to cover his debts. There are certain items of interest to the Heydonian, and we have room this year in our acquisitions budget, but everyone on the board of directors has something different in mind for the collections. We agreed on a dozen of the books and a few very interesting artifacts, but one of those has questions that have to be answered first: a bronze plaque with a disk of red carnelian set into it, Italian work, apparently very ancient. The Heydonian's arranged to receive it on loan until the estate is settled, and our people are trying to determine whether it's authentic or a modern forgery. Dr. O'Shaughnessy spent all day yesterday running tests on it. He's tolerably certain that it's as old as it appears to be."

"So, Roman?" Ariel guessed.

"Quite a bit older than that. It has three words written on it in the Faliscan language, one of the languages that was spoken in Italy before the Romans conquered the peninsula. It's one of a very modest number of Faliscan inscriptions that survives, and no one's certain what two of the words mean. The third is *hirpi*." After another sip of coffee: "You'll be interested to know that it means 'wolves.'"

Ariel nodded, then blushed a little, for her grandfather had gracefully avoided mentioning Nicodemus in her hearing for the entire time she'd lived with him.

"A remarkable item," he went on, "and there's apparently reason to think that it has a significant connection to certain very old traditions of magic. There were still Faliscan priests in Roman times who were called *Hirpi Sorani*, the wolves of the god Soranus. They had some remarkable powers. So it may be connected to that."

"Does anyone know how Harshaw got it?"

"That's the question that has to be settled. If he bought it from a dealer or collector that had it legally, that's one thing. If it was obtained illegally, that's quite another. In the first case the Heydonian certainly wants it for the museum collection. In the second case, it's stolen property no matter how many hands it's passed through, and it will be handed over to the heirs of the original owner, or to the Italian government if it was taken illegally from an archeological site. The Heydonian's policies are quite strict about stolen property, and of course there's more of that in the antiquities trade than anyone wants to admit. So it's necessary to trace the provenance and provenience of the piece before the Heydonian decides on a purchase, and to do it without word of the investigation getting into the media and risking a scandal if it turns out to be stolen. That's my job. Or, rather, our job."

Ariel's face lit up at the last two words. "You'll have to tell me what to do."

"Of course." With a wry look: "I'm sorry to say cases like this are on the duller end of my business. A little less exciting, in fact, than learning to scry in a crystal."

"Okay," said Ariel, grinning. "I can deal. How do you figure out the—" She stopped, tried to recall the words.

"Provenance and provenience. The first is the sequence of owners before the plaque came into Harshaw's possession. The second is the original source—an archeological site, for example. The first takes searching through catalogues from art auctions and private sales. Most of those are digitized nowadays, and the Heydonian has access, but it's still a slow process. The other? More searching through scholarly databases. We should be busy for several days at least."

"Are we going to start today?"

"Unless you had other plans."

"Nope. Let me grab my shoulder bag and I'm good."

He speared a kipper with his fork and said, "Not quite so fast. I do need a few more minutes to finish my breakfast." Ariel blushed, and used her coffee cup to cover the reaction.

It was close to an hour, with one thing and another, before Dr. Moravec's decades-old black Buick Riviera pulled into a parking space across the street from the massive white marble structure that housed the Heydonian Institution. "So, 1970," said Ariel as the car came to a stop.

"Exactly. If it was in private hands before then, it's not subject to current laws about the sale of antiquities." The engine sank into silence. "If it was in Europe during the Second World War, of course, that could land us in quite another round of problems. The Nazis stole a great many things from private collections, and not all of those got back to their rightful owners after the war. Most of them have been found, but—" He shrugged. "We'll see."

He got out of the car and Ariel did the same. "Remember," he said then. "Not a word about this to anyone. There are reporters who would be delighted to get a scandalous story about stolen artworks at the Heydonian." Ariel nodded, followed him toward the marble building.

The rain had stopped, but thick gray clouds scudded past not far overhead. Traffic stayed sparse as they walked across the street to the front entrance of the Heydonian. A colonnade of fluted pillars in white marble flanked the great bronze doors. Dr. Moravec opened one of these for Ariel, and followed her into the great echoing entrance hall: big as a house, with ornate lamps hanging on chains from a coffered ceiling high above, reflected in the polished gray stone of the floor. Portraits on one wall gazed benignly on a vast allegorical canvas on the other: Elias Ashmole, John Heydon, and the other founders of colonial Adocentyn being guided by a figure in Egyptian clothing to the doors of a great temple of golden stone.

Ariel let her grandfather take the lead once they were inside. As she expected, he headed straight back to the far end of the entrance hall and then through leather-covered doors into the reading room beneath the big central dome, where silence weighed down hard on great wooden tables and the handful of scholars who sat at them. Dr. Moravec nodded to the bald clerk in the ill-fitting brown suit who sat at the desk by the door, then led Ariel back past the tables to an inconspicuous door and through it into a smaller space. There, dark oak wainscoting with plaster walls above, light fixtures in brass sconces on the walls, and two windows with small diamond-shaped panes in ornate wooden frames clashed grievously with a long row of gray steel filing cabinets against one wall, and half a dozen Scandinavian-modern carrels lined up on the facing wall, each one flaunting a desktop computer and a screen.

"Here we are," said Dr. Moravec. "Let me get you into the computer system." A few quick flurries of keystrokes got one of the computers awake. "There you are. Every sale by one of the major auction houses here and in Europe in the last hundred years is at your fingertips. Do you remember the keywords we discussed?"

Ariel nodded and settled into the chair in front of the screen. It took her a few moments to figure out how to use the website her grandfather had accessed, but once she'd sorted it out she typed in the first set of search terms they'd discussed, and hit the enter button. The little light that showed the internet connection flickered, and the answer came back: *search term not found*. She rolled her eyes and went on to the next set. Meanwhile Dr. Moravec sat at the next computer over and began typing in sudden short bursts.

She was on the third set of terms when Dr. Moravec's cell phone rang, playing a snippet of classical music she didn't recognize. He answered, listened for a little while, and then said, "I'm in Room 104." Then: "That will be fine. I'll see you shortly." He hung up. Ariel glanced at him, kept hunting.

She was still busy with that when the door opened and a rotund man with a full white beard and little round glasses came through it. He wore a tweed jacket, brown woolen slacks, and a white shirt with the collar unbuttoned. He had a leather portfolio tucked under one arm, and reminded Ariel irresistibly of Santa Claus in the off season. "Bernard," he said, in a gruff voice with just a trace of Irish accent. "And you? I don't believe we've met."

It took Ariel a moment to realize that the last remark was directed at her. "Hi," she said, and got to her feet. "I'm Ariel Moravec."

"My assistant," Dr. Moravec added.

"Pleased to make your acquaintance. Terry O'Shaughnessy." He pressed Ariel's hand, released it. Then, to Dr. Moravec: "Anything yet?"

"We're just getting started."

Dr. O'Shaughnessy nodded. "I don't imagine this will help you at all, but something very interesting came back this morning from the lab. You've met Anna Martelli, right? She ran computer analyses on the reverse and found a second inscription in *notae Tironianae*."

Ariel tried to make sense of this, decided she'd have to ask her grandfather about it later. Some hint of that must have shown on her face, because Dr. O'Shaughnessy glanced at her, let out a little sniff, and said to her, "Sounds like Martian, I know. Here's the simple version. The back of the plaque's a fine mess, but someone scratched a message on it maybe two thousand years ago and one of our lab techs got a good image of it. *Notae Tironianae*, Tironian notes, are Roman shorthand. This is what it looks like if you pull the message out of the mess."

He opened the leather portfolio, handed her a color photograph printed on stiff paper. On it, pictured against a bland white background, was a five-sided object shaped a little like a child's drawing of a house. The grayish green color of weathered bronze, it was rough and heavily scratched, and had what looked like a small paper label glued to the upper right corner with C 117 written on it. Most of the scratches looked like the random results of centuries of wear and tear, but not all. Some of them had been traced out in white lines, showing odd jagged shapes that didn't look like any language Ariel knew.

"I didn't know the Romans did shorthand," she said.

"Most ancient peoples did," said Dr. O'Shaughnessy. "The alphabet we use now started out as ancient Egyptian shorthand. Faster to write than hieroglyphics. Some Roman collectors of art during the Empire used Tironian notes to mark things they owned."

She handed the photo to her grandfather, who studied it. "*C. Annaeus Crantor*," he said after a moment. "The name of the collector, presumably. The words below aren't so clear. Maybe it's just that the classes I took in Latin paleography were too long ago."

Dr. O'Shaughnessy snorted. "No doubt, but the state of the writing doesn't help. The first word begins *Sor-*, that's for certain. The middle's a fair mess, but *donum*'s likely enough. The last word begins with *ver-* something, but the rest of it is pretty well lost."

"I'll risk a guess on the first word," said Dr. Moravec.

"Oh, given the inscription on the front, the first two are almost certainly *Sorano donum*, 'gift to Soranus.' It's the last word that's the puzzle. *Vernali*, maybe, for a springtime festival, or *Vertumno*, if it was offered to Vertumnus and Soranus both. Or any number of other things."

Dr. Moravec nodded. "And the question of authenticity?"

"It seems likely at this point. The *notae* are in the style of the early Empire, with the sort of wear over the top of it a forger would have to work hard to fake, and the bronze is the proper chemical composition for an early Italic date. It's leaded bronze as it should be, not a bit of zinc in it—that's usually where forgers slip up, you know. Crantor's obscure, too, but he's known: one of the scholarly friends of Emperor Claudius. Not conclusive in the strict sense, but heading that way." He sent a glance Ariel's way, then, and handed her another photo on stiff paper. "Here's the thing we're talking about. What do you think of it?"

She gave him a startled look, then considered the photo. It was the same five-sided shape with the same green-gray patina, but a gleaming crimson disk filled the middle of it, like a full moon rising in a sky tinged with smoke. Three words in an alphabet she didn't know ran in a line close to the bottom of the piece. On each side, above the words, a stylized animal faced in toward the crimson disk, head raised. "Wolves howling at the moon," she said.

"Good!" Dr. O'Shaughnessy looked pleased. "That's my interpretation, certainly. The middle word's *Hirpi*—did Bernard tell you what that means? Very good. So we might just have a genuine artifact from the cult of the god Soranus on Mount Soracte. That's how it'll be labeled in the museum, certainly."

"The committee's decided to go ahead and exhibit it?" Dr. Moravec asked him. "That seems a little premature."

"Granted, but I don't doubt it'll happen so long as there isn't too much trouble with the provenance. Marjorie tells me the estate's agreed to extend the loan." To Ariel: "I imagine you've heard all about the big exhibition this winter." Ariel shook her head, and he went on. "*Artifacts of Ancient Magic*. Some of the exhibits are from the Heydonian collections, some are from museums all over the world. Have you heard of the Kynokefale machine?"

She shook her head.

"An astrological computer from Roman times, all gears and dials. It's one of only two in the world, and we'll have the original and a working reproduction on display. It'll be quite the spectacle. I don't recommend missing it." He nodded once, reclaimed the photos, and said, "I'll leave you to your work."

Once he was gone, Ariel sent a glance toward her grandfather. He responded with a slight impenetrable smile. She took the hint, sat down in front of the computer she'd been using, and started to enter another search string.

CHAPTER 3

FORMS OF INVISIBILITY

The next morning dawned brisk and blustery. The clouds overhead were shredded gray shapes driven by a wind that blew salt and strong off Cooper Bay. Ariel left home early, though not so early as her grandfather, and walked down Lyon Avenue most of the way to the old harbor. A block from the waterfront she turned onto Moon Street. From there, her route took her straight to a narrow storefront wedged between an urban hardware store and a downscale hair salon. The plate glass window next to the door had two neon signs in it. One, white and purple, showed an open eye surrounded by wavy rays, and below that, six words:

> AUNT CLARICE
> CLAIRVOYANT
> SHE SEES ALL

The other sign, vivid red, said simply OPEN. The door next to it, glass in a metal frame, followed through on the promise by swinging easily and letting her in.

The interior of the shop was familiar enough to Ariel to be comfortable, though it hadn't been that long since she'd first come there. Candles burning over on the left side of the store, on a long counter that served as a candle altar, splashed yellow light up to compete with the paler glow from the shop's ancient light fixtures, and put scents of hot wax and herbal oils into the air. Enameled steel shelves that looked salvaged from some earlier store filled the middle, holding up a considerable weight of candles, bottles, and trinkets. To the right were glass cases guarding the more expensive curios, with the sales counter tucked in toward the front of the shop. No one was visible anywhere inside, but as the door whispered shut behind her a familiar voice from further back said, "Good morning, Ariel."

"Good morning," she called out, and wove her way through the shelves to the alcove in back of the shop. Aunt Clarice was waiting there, perched on a chair at a round table just big enough for two to sit at: a tiny bird-boned old woman with dark brown skin and tautly curled silver hair spilling back from a headcloth of purple silk. Her dress, a deeper shade of purple, had a spray of gold stars spangled across it.

"Cassie's already in back," Aunt Clarice said. "That child's going to be fifteen minutes early to her own funeral. It'll be herbs again today—a batch of something quite interesting just came in the mail, and it has to be bagged. Later on we can talk about what it's good for. That'll keep us busy for the rest of the day."

Ariel thanked her. "Anything I need to take back?"

"Not a thing. I sent Cassie with all of it as soon as she got here." She got up and went to the little counter to one side of the alcove, got the teakettle heating up for the morning's readings. A shooing motion with one hand sent Ariel on her way. "You head on back. I'll be there in about a minute."

Ariel nodded and went to the door that led to the back room. The narrow passage into the back room didn't delay her long. She went through the door on the other side and said, "*Annyeong gom.*" The words were Korean, and they meant, "Hi, bear." She'd learned them from Cassie, a week or so after hearing the legend that traced Cassie's Korean ancestors back to an unusually devout member of that species.

Cassie, sitting at the long battered table that filled half the room, looked up from the tangled mass of plant matter she was extracting from a bag, and grinned. "*Annyeong ili.*"

Ariel had expected "*Annyeong ingan*," "Hi, human," and blinked. "What's *ili*?"

"Wolf. The way you howled Saturday night, you earned it."

"Okay," said Ariel, grinning back. "Thanks." She shed her coat and perched on a chair near Cassie's. "I have kind of a thing about wolves, ever since I was really young."

"Now surprise me," said Cassie. "Any chance you're descended from one?"

Ariel laughed. "I wish." Then, considering the unfamiliar plant in the big bowl between them, a tangle of dried fronds that looked like ferns: "So what's this stuff?"

"Fern seed," said Cassie.

Ariel gave her a dubious look. "I didn't think ferns had seeds."

"They don't," said Aunt Clarice, behind her. As usual, she'd made no noise coming into the room, but this time Ariel managed not to jump too visibly when she spoke. "Old-fashioned herbals call them that, but they're actually spores, as fine as powder. There'll be a good bit of it loose in the bag already, and the rest'll have to be brushed loose onto white paper and put in little bags. I'll show you how it's done in a bit."

"What's fern seed good for?" Ariel asked.

"It makes you invisible," the old woman said. Ariel gave her an uncertain look, trying to guess how seriously to take the words, and Aunt Clarice chuckled. "Not like in movies," she said then. "If you use it for magic, you'll still show up on camera, and if somebody knows how to pay attention, or you do something too obvious, oh, they'll see you all right. But fern seed helps keep people from noticing you. Most people don't notice half of what's around them anyway. This kind of magic just makes it a little easier for you to be the thing they don't notice. We'll talk about all that a little later on."

The fern fronds were dry and leathery, and they crackled as Ariel and Cassie pulled them out of the bowl one at a time. The process of extracting the spores from the little circular dots on the undersides of the leaflets was more complex than Ariel expected, and took a magnifying glass and a little stiff brush. Later on, Aunt Clarice explained a few of the things that could be done with fern spores in magic. The whole time Cassie took notes on her phone, thumbs dancing across the screen with practiced ease.

Ariel didn't have that option, by choice; her last smartphone had ended its existence by being snapped in half and dropped into the waters of Coopers Bay. That still counted as one of the best days of her life, and her shorthand studies were meant to make up the gap. Still, two months of practice hadn't taught her to take dictation as fast as the secretaries in her favorite 1920s mysteries, and she didn't always remember the shorthand symbols she needed. The pages she filled in her notebook that morning ended up as blotchy messes of shorthand squiggles and scrawled words. That annoyed her, since she knew she'd have to make a readable copy later.

Later on, as the morning wound down, Aunt Clarice had them make amulets—"tobies" was her term for them—for sale to the shop's customers. That involved inserting a carefully chosen mix of herbs into little red bags, tying them shut, and then putting them into plastic envelopes and stapling cardboard labels over the top to close them. As always, she had the two of them each take one for their own use.

"Tobies like these are good for protection," the old woman said. "Especially when people are trying to lie to you or fool you in some other way." She turned to Cassie. "You might want to give one to Orion. He's going to need it in a little while. You—" She turned to Ariel. "You should keep yours. You'll need it. Not right away, but fairly soon. Do you know a man with one eye?" Ariel shook her head, and Aunt Clarice went on: "If you meet someone like that any time in the next week or so, talk to him. He can set you straight about something you won't otherwise be able to find out about. Just something to keep in mind." She made a shooing motion with one hand. "Now you two get going. I've got a client coming in a few minutes, and I can tell she's going to be a real handful this time."

They thanked her, pocketed their tobies, said their goodbyes and went to the door. The rain had stopped, leaving the streets dark and gleaming. Torn gray clouds rushed past above the roofs of the tall brick buildings to either side of Moon Street. As the two of them walked toward Lyon Avenue, Ariel said, "I've got to go to the Heydonian this afternoon."

Cassie gave her a sidelong look. "Investigating something?"

"Yeah." Ariel made a face. "I spent all day yesterday sitting in front of a computer, trying to find something in a bunch of databases. Zero hits."

That got another look from Cassie, harder to read, and then a laugh. "You watch, you'll end up finding another pirate treasure. See you tomorrow."

She turned up Lyon Avenue and started up the hill. Ariel watched her go and then crossed the street. Cassie's reaction troubled her a little, but Aunt Clarice's comment about the one-eyed man held more of her attention. She searched back through the people she'd met since her move to Adocentyn, but none of them was missing an eye. She shook her head, went on.

Another block brought her to Flagler Way, which cut across the street grid at an angle, heading toward the Art Deco skyscrapers of Adocentyn's downtown. The wind came sweeping straight into her face as she turned that way, and she huddled into her coat and walked faster. Half a dozen blocks brought her to the town green with the old bronze statue of Elias Ashmole in the middle of it, and another few blocks past the statue, the white marble mass of the Heydonian loomed up. One of the bronze doors pivoted smoothly open for her, and she went through into the echoing entrance hall. To her surprise, someone she knew was approaching the doors from the other side at that same moment.

"Good afternoon, Ariel." A big man in every dimension, brown-skinned and muscular, Lieutenant Leo Jackson wore a camel-colored suit, a pink shirt, and a striped tie. Whenever she saw him, it startled Ariel a little to remember that his daughter Cassie was so short.

"Hi, Lieutenant Jackson. I hope you're not here on business."

"Unfortunately, yes. Someone tried to break into the building here last night." He shrugged. "Nothing like the first time that's been tried, of course. Your grandfather can fill you in on the details. Gotta run."

Startled, Ariel managed some kind of response, and he nodded and went out the door. She glanced after him, then shook her head and went on. The leather-covered doors of the reading room admitted her, and the bald clerk inside glanced at her visitor's card and made a note in his book. From there she went through the reading room to the little room with the computers and file cabinets.

Her grandfather was already there, sitting at one of the computers, scrolling through pages of text. He glanced up as she came into the room and said, "Good afternoon, Ariel. I trust your day has been more exciting than mine."

"I saw Lieutenant Jackson a minute ago. Something happened."

Dr. Moravec waved her to a seat at the computer next to his. "Oh, granted. Every few years someone tries to break into the Heydonian. That's no surprise, since we have quite a few valuable items in the collections, but our security systems are tolerably good."

"Magical ones?"

"Among others." He typed something on the keyboard in front of him and said nothing else for a moment. Just when Ariel was sure he wasn't going to say any more, he went on. "In this case something a little more conventional got in the way.

Whoever it was had some way of defeating the security cameras watching one of the doors, so their image didn't appear on the video while they picked the lock. There are silent alarms on every door, and those aren't easy to spot, but the person or people in question noticed the alarm sensor and got away before our security people arrived."

"So, no harm done," Ariel ventured.

"Except that nobody's sure why the cameras failed, and someone now knows more about our security systems than anyone outside the Heydonian has any business knowing." He allowed a shrug. "That was why Leo Jackson was here. I've also got a call in to someone I know at the FBI, in case we're dealing with a national or international theft ring. If they can match this with some known modus operandi that may make things a little easier for us."

Ariel nodded. "You know something funny? Aunt Clarice had us packaging fern seed this morning." That earned her a raised eyebrow from him, and she went on: "She said a camera will still take pictures of you when you use that, though."

"She's quite correct," said Dr. Moravec. "There's more than one way to avoid being seen."

He reached over and tapped a sequence of numbers on the keypad of the computer in front of her. The hard drive muttered to itself, the screen lit up, and a search screen she didn't recognize came up. "I finished searching the sales records just now," he said. "If the plaque was sold, none of the major art dealers or auction houses were involved. The next thing I'd like you to do is to check the files of exhibition catalogs and see if any museum in our databases put the plaque on display anywhere. A long shot, but it's worth doing before we start into the really dull part of the search."

"Okay," said Ariel. "What's that?"

"Printed catalogs from the smaller art dealers. Those are being digitized, but—" He shrugged again. "It's slow work and won't be finished for years. Most of them are still boxed up in storage rooms down in the basement. If it comes to that we'll have to have them sent up and go through them a box at a time."

Ariel nodded, and tried not to think about the prospect of spending months looking through one catalog after another. The screen in front of her made a helpful distraction. She tried one search string and then another, with no results worth noticing. A glance at her grandfather showed him deep in some other search, focused intently on the screen in front of him and entering little bursts of letters at intervals. Time went past, and she ventured more possibilities with no more success. After that she stared at the screen for a long moment, while her grandfather typed something else on his keyboard.

"That word for wolf," she said then. "The one on the plaque. What was it again?"

"*Hirpi.*" He spelled it aloud for her.

"Thanks." The keys clattered briefly beneath her fingers. The hard drive muttered. She waited for *search string not found* to pop up on the screen. To her surprise, she got instead a series of abbreviations and numbers that communicated nothing to her.

"Um." She pivoted to face him. "I got something but I'm not sure what it means."

Dr. Moravec leaned over, considered her screen. His eyebrows went up. "Interesting." He indicated the row of file cabinets with a gesture. "That would be uncommonly helpful if it's correct. Fourth cabinet, top drawer, the file labeled 1968."

She got up, went to the cabinet and extracted the file from among two dozen others. It contained half a dozen plump staple-bound booklets with stiff paper covers. Back at the carrel, she handed the file folder to him, and he flipped through the contents, handed her one, and said, "If the listing's accurate, the plaque will be in here."

Ariel took it. The cover was light brown and had the words ANCIENT ITALIAN MAGICAL ARTS printed on it in an old-fashioned font, and HEYDONIAN INSTITUTION in smaller type near the bottom. An exhibition catalog? That was her first guess, and a glance at the first few pages confirmed it: for six months in 1968, the Heydonian Museum had hosted a modest exhibit of early Italian occult artifacts in one of its rooms. She paged further on, past crisp black and white photos of lead curse tablets covered with incomprehensible writing, endearingly awkward little statues of household gods, a bronze liver used by novice diviners to learn how to read signs in the entrails of sacrificed sheep, and much more.

She turned another page, and her breath caught. There the plaque was, a good clear black and white photo of it, with the wolves howling on either side of the carnelian disk and the unfamiliar letters underneath. Under the photo was a little block of text in small print:

> **VOTIVE PLAQUE.** Etruscan or Faliscan, 6th century BC. Said to be connected to the Hirpi Sorani wolf cult of Mount Soracte. *Collection of Miss Leonora Blake.*

Without a word, she handed the catalog to her grandfather, who glanced at it and then at her. "Good," he said. "That was very capably done."

Ariel blushed. "Thanks. It was just a lucky guess."

"Clever rather than lucky, I would say." He paused, considering. "In fact, I think this calls for a late pizza lunch."

Startled, she still managed to clear her thoughts enough to answer promptly. "Double cheese and sausage?"

"Done. I'll put in a request for the file from that exhibition—it'll certainly be in the basement storage rooms. Once that's taken care of, we can leave."

Ariel tried to figure out the best way to ask the obvious question. Her grandfather glanced her way, and forestalled her. "You're wondering why a small celebration is in order. There are three reasons. First, I wasn't looking forward to spending months searching through old catalogs. Second, a

1968 exhibition means that the plaque was in private hands well before the current laws took effect, and that spares the Heydonian quite a bit of uncertainty and trouble. The plaque can certainly be part of the upcoming exhibit." He paused, and to her surprise, something almost wistful showed in his face. "But there's also a personal issue. I knew Leonora Blake rather well, back when I first came to Adocentyn. I wasn't aware that she owned the plaque, but it doesn't surprise me at all, and I'm glad to find out that she had it. Perhaps just a matter of nostalgia, but perhaps—" A smile even more impenetrable than usual veiled whatever emotion he'd shown so briefly. "Perhaps something more."

Chapter 4

A SHAPE IN THE DARKNESS

The Buick pulled into an open spot along Lyon Avenue's parking strip while the sky was still gray with fading afternoon light. Dr. Moravec had scarcely spoken a word since the two of them left the Heydonian. His face communicated even less than it usually did, but Ariel had begun to learn some of the subtler indications of his moods and guessed that some powerful emotion moved him. She watched him as closely as she could without being obvious about it, while they got out of the Buick and walked the few dozen steps to the door.

Once inside, Ariel went to get tea started while her grandfather picked up the phone. By the time he'd finished ordering the pizza, she'd left the kitchen and settled in her usual place on one side of the sofa. A pause after the order was placed told her that he was checking messages; a little after that, he dialed and made a call. Ariel glanced up, but she could hear only fragments of the conversation and got out the book on magic by Papus.

Her grandfather finished the call and came into the parlor. "We'll have a visitor in two hours or so," he said. "And quite possibly another case." He extracted his wallet, set a few bills on the coffee table.

Ariel set aside her book. "Berries. What's up?"

"We'll have to see. A Mr. Gerard Breyer, not someone I've met before, with questions about what I investigate and what rates I charge. He wasn't willing to discuss over the phone what kind of case he had in mind." He allowed a fractional shrug. "That's common enough with a certain kind of client."

"I can dust out once he gets here," said Ariel.

Dr. Moravec shook his head. "If this turns out to be something worth investigating I'll want your help. In the past I've tried to avoid taking more than one case at the same time, since it's not as easy as I'd like to be two places at once."

She waited for a raised eyebrow to signal that he meant the words as a joke, but didn't get it. Trying to guess what that meant was more than she wanted to face just then. "Let me know what you want me to do."

He nodded, said nothing more. Ariel watched him for a while and then went back to work trying to make sense of Papus's comments on magic. In due time the doorbell rang, and she left the couch, picked up the money, paid the delivery person, came back with a pizza in the traditional cardboard box and set it on an iron trivet on the coffee table. Extracting a slice each kept both of them busy for a little while. Finally, though, when she'd bitten off the point of her slice and swallowed, she said, "So tell me about Leonora Blake. She sounds interesting."

Her grandfather glanced at her, busied himself eating some of the pizza. Ariel waited. Once he'd swallowed and sipped tea he said, "She was. A most interesting person, in fact. She was one of the first people I met after I came here. I hadn't originally planned on staying in Adocentyn for more than a year or so. Meeting her changed that." He was silent for a moment, went on: "She was a very special person and I cared a great deal about her."

Ariel, astonished, opened her mouth and then closed it again. He studied the slice of pizza in his hand, took another bite, and washed it down with more tea before going on.

"Not in any romantic sense, mind you. She was thirty years my senior, and a confirmed spinster. Besides, what happened with your grandmother was still very much on my mind in those days, and romance was quite literally the last thing I wanted to cope with. But she was one of the two closest friends I had in those days, and the other was the one who introduced me to her."

"Theophilus Cray."

"Exactly."

He busied himself eating pizza for a while. Ariel had almost given up hope of hearing more about the subject from him, when he finished his slice, leaned back in his chair, and began to talk. "Leonora lived in a one-bedroom apartment a few blocks east of the Heydonian, in a pleasant old building—demolished twenty years ago, I'm sorry to say. She'd been living there for many years, since long before I first came to Adocentyn. She slept on a folding bed in the parlor because the bedroom was entirely given over to magic. Six days a week she would go to the Heydonian reading room to study books on magic, and every Sunday she attended an odd little church out on West Randolph Avenue, gone now as well, which I visited a few times.

"She was a writer in her younger days, though not a very successful one. As I recall, she published three novels and five books of poetry. None of them brought in much money, so she lived on her inheritance and ran up considerable debts once inflation started cutting into that. Once she died, her entire estate had to be sold off to pay her bills. It's quite possible that's how Harshaw came by the plaque, of course, and that's something I'll be able to check on."

Ariel considered that while she extracted another slice of pizza from the box. "Do you think I'd like her books?"

"You might," said her grandfather. "I'm no judge of poetry, and I don't believe we've discussed your taste in verse, but as I recall, I thought her novels were tolerably good. I couldn't tell you much about them now, as it's been too many years. I once had copies of all her books, but—" He allowed a fractional shrug. "Fiction's never been a great interest of mine, and once Leonora was gone I gave my copies to friends who I thought would appreciate them."

Ariel nodded.

"Most of what drew us together was a common interest in certain kinds of magic—that, and the fact that we found each other very congenial. We used to meet for lunch now and then, and once she decided she could trust me, I went to her apartment for certain kinds of magical training. I'll be passing those on to you, if you're interested, once you've completed the necessary preparations."

"Thank you."

He nodded, acknowledging. "I don't pretend that I learned all her secrets. She had a great many of those, and only a certain fraction had to do with magic. Theophilus also knew her quite well—better than I did, in fact, since they were related—but I doubt he knew everything about her either. He called her Aunt Leonora, though I think they were technically third cousins. The two of us gave her a certain amount of help during her final illness, along with people from her church, and it so happened that I was the one who drove her to the hospital when the chest pains told us both her heart had begun to fail."

He fell silent, considered the remains of the pizza. Ariel watched him for a while, then said, "You really did care about her a lot."

"She was a very remarkable person." He extracted another slice from the box, used it as an excuse for silence. Ariel considered saying something else, decided against it. Over the minutes that followed, as they finished the pizza, she brooded over her grandfather's comments. In the months since she'd come to Adocentyn, he'd mentioned events in his past fewer than a dozen times, and most of those had been brief cryptic references to people she didn't know and happenings she'd never heard about. Never before had he talked more than briefly about his friendships, and the way he'd spoken of his feelings about Leonora Blake left her feeling as though she'd just watched the sun rise in the west.

Once lunch was finished, she got up and carried the pizza box out to the trash can in the kitchen, came back with another cup of tea. Though she hadn't heard so much as a whisper of movement, he'd left the living room, and the door to his study clicked softly shut a moment later. That didn't surprise her at all. A glance at the largest dial on the grandfather clock showed that she still had time before the arrival of Gerard Breyer and his mystery, whatever that turned out to be. She settled back on the sofa and went to work on the next chapter of the book by Papus.

She'd finished the chapter and started studying her notes from the last few days of work at Aunt Clarice's when the strange old clock in the parlor sounded the hour. As the last chime rang out, the doorbell buzzed. Ariel plopped her notebook on the end table and went to the front door. She glanced through the peephole for form's sake, saw a middle-aged man standing on the steps, and opened the door.

"Good afternoon," said the man, in a baritone voice. "I'm Gerard Breyer. I have an appointment with Dr. Moravec." He was in his fifties, perhaps, short, compact, and muscular, with black hair and a broad mustache just beginning to go gray. He wore brown slacks and a cream-colored cable knit sweater; his shoes, brown leather oxfords with heavy soles, had seen plenty of wear. His face caught Ariel's attention hardest, though. Lean and angular, it looked as though every scrap of spare flesh had been whittled away from the bones, leaving hard angles to frame a lean hooked nose and eyes so dark brown they looked black.

Ariel stepped out of the way, said "Please come in," and closed the door after him.

By then, as she'd expected, her grandfather had come out of his study. "Mr. Breyer?"

"Dr. Moravec." They shook hands. "Thank you for being willing to meet with me on such short notice. This whole situation is—" A gesture indicated bafflement. "Not the kind of thing I'm used to at all."

"Of course." Dr. Moravec motioned toward the parlor. "If you'd like to have a seat and tell me the details."

By then Ariel was in her place on the sofa, sitting in a slightly less casual posture than usual, with a stenographer's pad open and a pen in her hand.

"My assistant Ariel," Dr. Moravec said. "I trust you won't mind if she takes notes."

"Not at all." Breyer sat in an armchair close to the grandfather clock. Dr. Moravec settled in his usual chair, folded his hands and waited.

"I'll spare you the usual chatter about how this can't be happening, I must be going insane, all the rest of it," said Breyer. "I've had such thoughts, of course, but I'm not prepared to deny the evidence of my senses, and an acquaintance of mine—I'm not sure if you recall him, his name is Walter Krebs—"

"Yes, I do. He had difficulties with a very troublesome ghost."

"That's the one. He told me that you were the one person he knew about who might be able to help me."

"That's gratifying to hear," said Dr. Moravec. "And the difficulty you're facing?"

"Something's stalking me. Not all the time. Once a month, though, when I walk home from my office downtown, something follows me, something that looks like a shadow. It's shaped like a large dog, more or less, but it's jet black and practically featureless except for eyes, and I've seen it go right through a thick shrubbery and not disturb a single leaf. So far it hasn't done anything but follow me, watching me the whole time, but I'm concerned that it may get other ideas sooner or later. One way or another, I want to know what it is, why it's watching me—and what I have to do to get rid of it."

Dr. Moravec nodded. "Understandably. I'll need more details, however. You mentioned that you walk home from your office. Where is the office, where is your home, what route do you use, and when and why do you walk it?"

"Fair enough," said Breyer. "My office is in the Gorman Tower downtown. My house is at 1336 Zephon Place. The route varies, but it's usually more or less direct, especially after dark. I walk to and from work five or six days a week. I have a fairly sedentary job and the walk is part of how I keep from going to seed."

"And when did you last see the thing following you?"

"Last Saturday. I don't always go in on weekends but this autumn's been a busy time at work. On the way home, the thing started following me a block or so after I started along Warden Street and stayed with me all the way to my front door. It was still there a few minutes later, but it left shortly after that. I didn't see it go."

"I see. And the sighting before that? When did that happen?"

Breyer tilted his head to one side, frowned, and then pulled a little leather-covered notebook from a pocket and paged through it. "The seventeenth of last month," he said. "And the time before that—" He paged further. "September 19th. I'd have to check my diaries to go back any further, but I'm sure I saw it once in August."

"In the next day or so," said Dr. Moravec, "please write me out an account of every time you observed the thing watching you: date, time, place, route, every other detail you recall or happened to write down at the time. Send that to me as soon as it's complete."

"You'll have it in a day or two."

"Thank you. You mentioned that you live on Zephon Place. Perhaps you can tell me approximately when your house was built."

"I'm not sure," said Breyer. "It's old, I know that much. Most of the houses in that neighborhood are wood frame bungalows, but my place is stone. The realtor who sold it to me in 2009 said that it was the carriage house from an old estate. I don't know whether he was telling the truth, of course."

Dr. Moravec nodded again. "Very well. I have one more question, which you may not want to answer. I need to know whether you or anyone in your family has any connection with occultism, with old superstitions or traditions, or anything of that kind."

"Not that I've ever heard," Breyer said, frowning. "Certainly I've never gotten into that kind of thing. I have an aunt who knows the family traditions, though, and I'll give her a call this evening and see what she has to say."

"That would be very helpful. Is there anything else you can tell me?" Breyer shook his head, and Dr. Moravec went on: "In that case, perhaps you'd like to take care of the retainer and the advance on expenses, and we can proceed."

A checkbook promptly appeared, and Breyer filled out a check for a comfortable sum and handed it over. "Thank you," he said. "Partly for taking the case, but also for listening to me without treating me like some kind of nut."

"You're welcome. Maybe someday our society will learn how to put a little less effort into ignoring uncomfortable realities. Until it does—" He shrugged. "I have employment."

The usual polite words got exchanged, and Ariel walked Breyer to the door and closed it behind him. When she returned to the parlor, her grandfather had leaned back in his armchair and seemed to be pondering something located on the far side of the ceiling.

"Interesting," he said after a few moments. "What did you think of him?"

"I'm not sure he told you everything he knows," said Ariel.

"Good. No, almost certainly not." With a little shrug: "That's common enough. That said, this promises to be an interesting case. What does last Saturday have in common with the other two dates he mentioned?"

Ariel frowned and then admitted, "I don't know."

"The moon was full on each of those nights."

He met her incredulous look with his most impenetrable expression, and got up from the armchair. "Which means that I have research to do." He nodded once, turned, and went into his study, leaving Ariel to stare after him.

Chapter 5

A BONE OF CONTENTION

Dr. Moravec spent all that evening brooding over big leatherbound books in Latin, and the next morning told Ariel that he would be at the Heydonian until late and not to expect him for dinner. After more than five months under his roof, she was used to that, and simply nodded and poured herself more tea. Nine o'clock found her at Aunt Clarice's shop on Moon Street, where she and Cassie Jackson learned the proper way to apply oils and herbs to candles—dressing the candles, Aunt Clarice called that process—and then practiced it under the old woman's watchful gaze until they could both do it right. Clients came into the shop nearly every day to have Aunt Clarice do candle spells for them, and Ariel knew she'd be helping to cast those spells in due time. She took copious if messy notes on the process and thought about which of them she might cast for herself someday.

That evening she had the house on Lyon Avenue all to herself. She read another chapter of Papus and did her shorthand homework, then spent the hours that remained reading a Dashiell Hammett detective novel under the familiar gaze of the little wooden crocodile. Dr. Moravec still hadn't returned when she went upstairs, spent five not especially productive minutes trying to relax and five more waiting in vain for something to appear in the crystal, and went to bed.

The next morning he was finishing his breakfast when she first came downstairs, and asked her, "Will you be going to Clarice's today?"

"Nope. She's got too many readings on the schedule today and tomorrow both."

He nodded. "In that case perhaps you can do me a favor. I told the board yesterday what we found. The plaque's certainly going to be part of the exhibit, but before the Heydonian can make an offer on it we need a more complete provenance. That means learning how Harshaw came by it. His sister Holly lives here in Adocentyn, and I think she might be more willing to talk to you than to me. Perhaps you'd be willing to ask her a few questions about the plaque."

"Sure," said Ariel. "Do you have her number?"

"I'll get all the information for you before I leave." An hour later, as he went out the door and started for the Heydonian, she reviewed the phone number, the photo of the plaque, and the list of questions he'd given her, called on the land line in the kitchen, and got a youngish male voice on the other end. Holly Harshaw wasn't willing to discuss the matter over the phone, it turned out, but after several long pauses Ariel got an appointment for two in the afternoon.

The address she'd been given was an easy walk from their house, less than a block north of Culpeper Park. Ariel gave herself plenty of time to get there anyway. She considered walking through the park, since it was narrow at that end, but the weather had turned wet again overnight and the risk of getting to the Harshaw house with mud all over her shoes was not one she wanted to take. Instead, she went around the west end of the park, staying on sidewalks the whole way, with the great bare oaks rising up on her right like clawed hands trying to catch the gray unsettled sky. Cars grumbled by, and a cold wind came tumbling past the downtown skyscrapers a mile or so away to shove the unkempt grass flat and stir wet leaves around the trunks.

1164 Ithuriel Place turned out to be a big house from the turn of the previous century with a mansard roof, gray clapboard siding, pillars flanking the ornate front door, and lace curtains in decent condition visible in the windows. A glance at the pocket watch she kept in her purse, a thrift store find, showed two minutes to two: close enough, Ariel decided, and climbed the three steps to the door. The doorbell made a muffled discordant sound somewhere inside when she pushed the button. She waited, and after a minute or so the door rattled and opened.

"Yes?" A young man in jeans and a baggy green sweatshirt stood there, blocking the door. His voice was the one she'd heard on the phone. Curly brown hair and black-rimmed glasses framed a light brown face with pink-white blotches sprawled across it. The hand that held the door open was similarly blotched.

"Good afternoon," Ariel said, trying to sound as professional as she could. "I'm Ariel Moravec, Dr. Moravec's assistant. I have an appointment with Ms. Harshaw."

He considered her, then nodded. "Just a minute. You can hang up your coat there." He stepped out of the way, let her into the entry, and motioned toward one side of the room, where a big ornate coat tree waited. As she shed her coat and put it on one of the hooks, he closed the front door and then went somewhere further within.

A few moments passed while Ariel glanced around. Besides the coat tree, the entry featured an umbrella stand and a tile floor. Two paintings of mountain landscapes in impressively ugly gilt frames hung on the walls, clashing with the faded green wallpaper. The light fixture overhead looked like someone had tried to imitate a chandelier but didn't quite know how. She'd turned her attention to what little she could see of the parlor further in when she heard the young man's voice saying, "Mom? It's for you." The voice that answered was too low for Ariel to hear.

The young man returned. "Come with me," he said, turned his back and walked away. Ariel followed him across a big parlor cluttered with Victorian furniture and through a narrow hallway with more paintings on the walls to a room in back. It had rose-colored wallpaper on three walls; the fourth was mostly tall windows looking out onto a bedraggled back yard. A sofa upholstered in worn red velvet and flanked with ornate end tables faced the windows. An assortment of ladderback chairs, no two of them in the same style, occupied other bits of space.

On the sofa was a woman in her forties in a drab brown house dress and a white cardigan. She had the same curly brown hair as her son, but a rounder face, light skin with freckles but no blotches, and watery blue eyes that bulged out a little, giving her a popeyed look. She glanced up from a book as Ariel came into the room, considered her for a moment, and put the book away.

"Ms. Harshaw?" Ariel asked. She had to fight to keep her immediate reaction off her face, because Holly Harshaw looked far too much like her late brother for comfort.

"Yes." The woman's voice was deeper than Ariel expected, and a little rough. "You're Moravec's granddaughter, I suppose. Go ahead and have a seat." She waved vaguely at some of the ladderback chairs. Then, turning to the young man: "Thank you, Kyle." He nodded and left without saying another word.

Ariel perched on one of the chairs. "Thank you for being willing to talk to me."

That got her a brief unreadable look, nothing more.

"The thing I need to ask you about is this." She opened her purse, took out the photo of the bronze plaque, handed it to Holly Harshaw. "It belonged to your brother. The Heydonian's interested in buying it but they have to know the provenance and the provenience, of course. Do you recognize it?"

Ms. Harshaw looked up from the photo. Her face had tensed. "Yes. Yes, of course it would be that."

The reaction startled Ariel, though she did her best not to let it show. "Do you know how your brother got it?"

"It was Father's. Clarence inherited it when Father died in 2006."

Ariel had already gotten out her stenographer's pad and pen by then, and noted that down. "Thank you. That's something we didn't know and it helps." Then: "Do you know anything about how your father got it?"

Ms. Harshaw opened her mouth to speak, then shut it. "No," she said a moment later. "No, I don't know anything about that."

Another note went onto the pad. "That's okay."

"No, it isn't." When Ariel gave her an uncertain look: "This whole business isn't okay and it's never going to be okay."

Ariel waited a moment and then said, "If it's something you don't want to talk about, you don't have to, you know."

That got her a sudden wary look and a long silence. Finally: "No. It's just that I was supposed to get the plaque, but Father changed his will." She shrugged, forced a laugh. "One of those stupid family things that you wish you could forget. Father got it years ago. You know those are wolves on it, I imagine. Wolves howling at the moon. I liked wolves when I was a girl, and I fell in love with the plaque as soon as I saw it. But some things happened, family matters, nothing that you need to hear about, and the will got changed. So that and some other things went to Clarence instead, and now the paper says it's being bought by the Heydonian. I'm sure they'll tuck it into one of their vaults and nobody will ever see it again."

A pause went by. "What I've heard," Ariel said then, "is that it's going to be on exhibit in the museum this winter."

Ms. Harshaw glanced up at her, and made herself smile. "Well, that's something," she said. "I'll look forward to seeing it, then." She didn't sound as though she looked forward to it. She sounded as though she would rather be roasted alive on a griddle.

Ariel nodded, wondered what kind of tangled family issue she'd stumbled into, and tried to think of other questions that might be relevant. "Your brother," she said finally. "Did he ever say anything to you about the plaque?"

That got a laugh, and this time it wasn't forced. It was sharp-edged and brittle as broken glass. "Oh, yes. Not just once, either. Over and over again. But it didn't have anything to do with where the plaque came from. No, not at all. You didn't know my brother, did you?"

"I met him once," said Ariel, taken aback. "Dr. Moravec introduced us."

"In that case he was on his best behavior, I'm sure." The same brittle laugh set Ariel's teeth on edge. "Just one of our charming little family habits. You wouldn't understand." She got to her feet suddenly, turned toward the doorway and called out "Kyle?" Then, to Ariel: "I'm sorry I don't know anything that can help you."

Footsteps murmured in the hallway. Ariel stood up. "My parents took some things away from me that mattered a lot," she said, "and I like wolves, too. So maybe I understand a little." The words were a waste of breath, and she knew as much as she said them, but Holly Harshaw gave her a startled look and half opened her mouth, as though considering saying something.

Kyle came back into the room a moment later, though, and whatever it was went unsaid. "Show Ms. Moravec to the door," she told him, and then sat down and opened her book again, to signal that the conversation was at an end. Ariel glanced at her and then at Kyle, shrugged mentally, and let him lead her back through the hall and the parlor to the entry.

He paused before opening the front door. "It's about the plaque with the wolves on it, isn't it?" Once she had her coat back on, Ariel nodded, and he shook his head, made a little rough noise in his throat she couldn't interpret, and opened the door for her.

A moment later the door clicked shut behind her. That left her on Ithuriel Place under gray uncertain skies, with the great oaks of Culpeper Park looming up gray and leafless on the street's other side. She turned to retrace her route around the west end of the park, then stopped, crossed the street and considered the landscape ahead of her. At that point, Culpeper Park was only four blocks wide, and parts of it were grassy lawns and brick walkways beneath the great oaks, though other parts were thick with shrubs whose names Ariel didn't know. She could see Crown Street and the houses on its far side here and there under the trees. She reminded herself that it didn't matter if she got home with muddy shoes, and set off across the park.

The grass was wet, the fallen leaves were wetter, and the ground under them had turned soft with rain. After a few unsteady steps that nearly landed her face first in the grass, Ariel veered over to the nearest brick walkway and stayed on it, though it took her well out of her way as it looped around trees and benches. The great oaks spread skeletal limbs above her. Below, patches of mud added their own colors here and there to the symphony of grass and leaves. One of them, in a corner of the park close to an impenetrable thicket of shrubbery, had dog pawprints crossing it: a big dog, Ariel guessed, the size of a large German shepherd. If she'd seen the tracks in the woods, she decided, she might have thought they were the pawprints of wolves. She shook her head, chuckled at the absurdity of wolves in the middle of a city Adocentyn's size, then remembered Gerard Breyer's story and gave the tracks an uneasy look before she went on.

The path she was on seemed determined never to reach the sidewalk on the far side of the park, but finally it swung close enough that half a dozen cautious, squelching steps across the sodden grass got her there. A block along Crown Street brought her to the upper end of Lyon Avenue, and another half a block saw her home.

The mail had arrived by the time she got there. She scooped four envelopes and a sale flyer from a local grocery out of the box and brought them inside with her. Her coat went onto the coat tree, her wet shoes went onto the entry floor, the mail found its way to the parlor coffee table, and then she went upstairs to change into more comfortable clothes.

Only after she came back down and got tea started did she sit down on the couch and sort through the mail. All of the envelopes were addressed to her grandfather. One was the monthly water bill, another was a letter from something called the Heptasophic Order, the third was from Gerard Breyer, and the fourth was a square envelope of rose-colored paper with a return address she didn't recognize, in a handwriting she was certain she ought to remember. She set them back on the coffee table and got to work writing out the details of her visit with Holly Harshaw.

Time passed. She'd downed two cups of tea, done her day's shorthand lesson, buried herself in another Dashiell Hammett novel and turned on a lamp to chase off the gathering darkness when the door rattled and Dr. Moravec came in. "Good evening," he said once he'd shed his coat. "I'm glad to say I have some good news."

"About Mr. Breyer's shadow?"

A quick shake of the head dismissed the suggestion. "No, that's going to have to wait until I have more details."

Without a word, she extracted the envelope from Breyer from the rest of the letters and held it out to Dr. Moravec. He took it, nodded, and said, "Excellent. The good news relates to our other case. The files from the 1968 museum exhibit include a provenance for the bronze plaque. Leonora bought it in 1949 from a Spanish antiquities dealer, who obtained it the previous year from a collector in Madrid who'd had it since 1924, and he got it from an Italian aristocratic family in the Romagna who had it since sometime in the sixteenth century. I have some inquiries under way to be sure that the provenance is legitimate, but unless Harshaw came by it in some questionable way, the Heydonian should be able to buy it."

"Okay, good," said Ariel. "I can tell you something about how Harshaw got it."

"Let me get tea and you'll have my complete attention. A refill for you?"

She handed over her cup, went back to her notes for the few minutes it took Dr. Moravec to get tea prepared. Once he was in his chair with a teacup in hand, and invited her account with a gesture, she described as exactly as she could her conversation with Holly Harshaw.

"Very interesting," he said once she was finished. "It'll be easy enough to get Jasper Harshaw's will. He lived and died here in Adocentyn, so the county courthouse downtown will have it. Leonora's will should be there, too. Perhaps you'd be willing to learn one of the less exciting parts of the investigator's trade."

Ariel laughed. "I think you mean another of the less exciting parts. Of course."

"Thank you. You have tomorrow free, as I recall. Would a visit to the courthouse be an option, do you think?"

"Sure. Just let me know what to do."

"Of course." He opened the envelope from Breyer then, unfolded three sheets of paper from inside. "This is admirable," he said after a moment. "Not all clients are this organized." He leaned forward and held out the papers. Ariel took them and glanced over them: a crisp timeline of encounters with a black shadow that looked like a big dog, each entry detailing time, place, and the shadow's actions.

By the time she'd finished reading the account, Dr. Moravec had gathered up the rest of the mail. The water bill got a cursory glance. The letter from the Heptasophic Order got more attention, and he put the letter back in the envelope and slipped both into an inside pocket of his jacket without a word. The card in the rose-colored envelope was the only one that earned a raised eyebrow. He opened the envelope, extracted a card with an ornate floral design on it, read whatever was inside it, then opened something else that had been folded up in the card. That got a quizzical look, and then he handed the card and its contents to Ariel without a word.

She took it. One glance inside the card reminded her whose handwriting it was. Teresa Kozlowski—no, she reminded herself, Teresa Benedetti now. The wedding had been just a month back, and Ariel and her grandfather had been there, two out of a hundred or so guests in the big echoing church on Garibaldi Street, watching the end of another tangled case.

Thank you both so much for coming to our wedding, Teresa had written in the card. *Phil and I got back from our honeymoon on Tuesday and heard Wednesday that the auction was over.* Ariel nodded, recalling a story in the *Adocentyn Mercury* about the auction and the improbably large sum that Captain Curdie's long-rumored treasure had fetched. *We'd decided already that the two of you deserved some share of the proceeds, since it was your work that told Phil where to look for it, and the auction brought in so much. Please accept the enclosed with our profound thanks.* Their signatures followed.

The folded thing inside the card was a check. Ariel opened it, goggled, read it again, and then looked up at her grandfather. "Wow."

He nodded. "Ten thousand dollars isn't quite the most lavish gift I've received from a client, but it's close." He considered her, raised one eyebrow. "It occurs to me, though, that you did approximately half the work on that case. I trust you can find something to do with five thousand of it."

She goggled again, opened her mouth, closed it, and then said in a voice that squeaked: "Yeah." Then, mastering herself: "Thank you. That's really nice of you."

"You're entirely welcome. Perhaps I should do what my grandfather used to do when I was small and he gave me some money. He'd always tell me not to spend it all in one place."

Ariel considered that and beamed, realizing that a project she'd had in mind for months had just come within reach. "I won't. But I'll be spending some of it."

"What do you have in mind?"

"A camera. The old-fashioned kind that uses film."

He nodded, as if it were the most obvious thing in the world. "You might want to talk to Theophilus about that. He's a very capable photographer, among many other things."

"Okay." Then, more tentatively: "Should I call him?"

"That won't be necessary. He'll be coming over tomorrow evening. We have certain things to discuss." He allowed a fractional smile. "But I'm quite sure he'd be willing to talk photography as well."

Ariel considered the prospect and said, "Okay. But I should probably reread that book of Edward Lear's nonsense poems, then."

"Oh, quite possibly," said Dr. Moravec. "If you do, however, it's very likely he'll have some other bee in his bonnet. Theophilus is—" He allowed a shrug. "Theophilus."

Chapter 6

IN COLD PURSUIT

The county courthouse in downtown Adocentyn was a big Art Deco structure from the 1930s, all beige-tinted concrete, oddly spaced windows, and half-abstract human figures on the two big pilasters that flanked the front entrance. A flight of steps rose up to the door, paralleled on one side by an awkwardly placed wheelchair ramp. Inside, mustard-colored walls and linoleum flooring in an uneasy gray-and-brown swirl pattern made it abundantly clear that the taxpayers hadn't had to cover the costs of remodeling the place since the days when Dr. Moravec wore love beads and bell-bottom trousers. A directory on a wall close to the entrance, the kind with little white letters pressed into a grooved background covered in cheap black velvet, directed her to the back of the ground floor. There she found an open doorway leading into a bleak little room with a counter across its midsection.

On the far side of the counter, a short plump man in a cheap blue suit sat reading a book. He looked up at Ariel through wire-framed glasses as she came in, but said nothing and turned back to his book. She considered that, walked up to the counter, waited until he looked up again, and said, "Hi. I'd like to get copies of two wills."

"Probated?"

"Yes, both of them, a long time ago."

He put the book aside, reached under the counter, got out two copies of a blurry photocopied form and handed them to her without a word. She thanked him, extracted a pen and a spiral note pad from her shoulder bag, filled out the first copy and handed it back. The man in the blue suit glanced at it, then started typing on a keyboard. After an interval a printer over in the far corner of the room wheezed, groaned, cleared its mechanical throat, and began to spit out sheets of paper one at a time.

Ariel finished the second form and handed it over. "This one was—" It took her a moment to remember the term Dr. Moravec had used. "An insolvent estate. If you've got any information on what happened with it I'd like to get that too."

Again, he took it without a word, and started typing. The printer made noises that sounded uncomfortably like rhythmic gagging, but sheets of paper kept emerging. The man in the blue suit typed for a while, and then without looking up at her said, "Alcock."

"Excuse me?"

"Alcock." When she showed no sign of recognizing the word: "Alcock Estate Sales. That's who handled it."

Ariel thanked him. A scrap of memory surfaced: a sign she'd seen on the way to the courthouse. "Aren't they somewhere nearby?"

"Yeah. 413 Meacham. Right around the corner."

She thanked him again, paid the copying fee, tucked a stack of paper half an inch thick into her shoulder bag, and headed out the door into the corridor. Just then a bland, balding little man huddled into a heavy black woolen coat came along the same corridor, evidently headed for the office Ariel had just left. Brown eyes in a soft vague face, given a little more definition by round-framed glasses, glanced at her, blinked as if uncertain, looked elsewhere.

Ariel threaded her way back through the corridors of the courthouse and trotted down the stairs into the cold gray morning feeling pleased with herself. It took her two false starts before she found Meacham Street, but once that difficulty was past it didn't take long before she was standing outside the narrow shop front she'd passed earlier that morning, with ALCOCK ESTATE SALES in faded gold lettering on the window.

Inside, a cramped front office with cheap wood paneling on the walls made room grudgingly for two padded chairs, a table with a few outdated magazines on it, an office desk with an old computer perched on top, and a secretary on a swivel chair behind that. She wore a frosted blonde wig, thick makeup, and a dark blue jacket and skirt that had been fashionable before Ariel was born. She glanced up, startled, when Ariel came through the door, but recovered after an instant. "Good morning. May I help you?"

"I hope so," said Ariel. "I'm wondering if you have any records from an estate sale you handled in 1998."

"Yes, of course. Can I ask why you want to see them?"

She'd discussed that with her grandfather earlier, and didn't have to hesitate. "I work for Dr. Bernard Moravec at the Heydonian. He's looking into the provenance of an artwork the Heydonian is thinking about buying."

"Ah. I see." She did something with the keyboard on her desk, considered the screen, and then said, "Yes, we have all the records from that year in back. Why don't you give me the details and I'll see what I can get you. There'll be a copying fee, of course."

"Sure," said Ariel. "The estate belonged to Leonora Blake. I can give you the date she died and the docket number from the courthouse if you need that."

"No, not a bit. I'll need your name and—Dr. Moravec, was it?" Ariel gave her name. Another burst of typing, another glance at the screen, and the secretary got up. "Why don't you have a seat," she said. "This may take a little while."

Ariel settled on one of the chairs while the secretary left the room. After five minutes or so, from the sounds that came from further back, an office copier got to work on something. In due time it fell silent, and the secretary reappeared with a stack of papers in her hands.

"Somebody else wanted to know about this same sale," she said as she reached her desk. "We made another copy of this file last week."

Startled, Ariel managed to keep that reaction from showing. "I wonder if it's anybody I know," she said.

"Can't help you there," said the secretary. "We log every time somebody asks for a record, but names and companies are private. All I can tell you is somebody paid for them."

Another copying fee changed hands, another set of polite words got exchanged, and then Ariel put the sale records into her shoulder bag next to the will and went out onto the street again. A glance at her watch showed that the whole process had taken less time than she'd expected. She considered heading home right away, decided against it.

Instead, she paused to get her bearings, and started weaving her way through the streets of downtown Adocentyn. They were emptier than usual that morning, just a few pedestrians here and there bundled in warm coats against the raw wet November wind. A few cars rattled past, a county bus breathed diesel fumes at all and sundry as it rolled by. Ariel set a brisk pace and kept an eye on the gargoyles and carved faces up above street level, the one reliable guide she'd found to the tangled streets of the downtown district. Once or twice she had the uncomfortable feeling that someone was watching her, but the feeling passed as she hurried on.

In due time the main branch of the public library came in view, a huge Egyptian Revival structure of sand-colored stone. The first time she'd seen it, she'd wondered for a moment if it was a hallucination, and subsequent visits hadn't changed the reaction much. The two sphinxes that gazed down on Commerce Street with heavy-lidded eyes, the two colossal statues of hawk-headed gods flanking the bronze main doors, the soaring facade above and to both sides of the door with paired windows and a cornice of lotus blossoms six stories above, all seemed weirdly disconnected from the ordinary commercial buildings to either side, as though the city had grown up all anyhow around a pharaoh's tomb.

Passing through the doors brought Ariel back to some semblance of ordinary reality, or as close to that as fluorescent lights, beige steel shelves, and patrons who didn't look even slightly Egyptian could manage to convey. She rode the escalators up one after another to the fourth floor, where a squabble years back between a long-departed library administrator and Adocentyn's library patrons had stranded most of the older volumes in the collection. The Unpopular Fiction section, Cassie Jackson liked to call it; Ariel visited it regularly in search of the old novels she liked. This time she had something more specific in mind.

A tangled bit of local politics had kept the fourth floor collection from finding its way into the library's online catalog. That meant that an old-fashioned card catalog in brown wooden cabinets lined up along one wall provided the only guidance. Even so, it took Ariel less than a minute to find the right drawer and chase down the name she wanted, and another minute more weaving through the stacks brought her to the right shelf. A short thick volume in an old-fashioned cloth library binding waited there; its title was *The Chapel of the Grail*, and it had *Blake* stamped on the spine down below the title. She pulled it off the shelf, glanced at the title page to be sure it was by Leonora Blake, flipped through the pages briefly, and then took it with her back down the elevators to the librarians' desk on the first floor, the only place the old books could be checked out.

That was her last errand downtown that day. The wind hadn't gotten any warmer, and she pulled her coat tight around her and kept up a fast pace as she started for home. The traffic lights had their own ideas of a suitable rate of speed, though, and several times she had to stand on an otherwise empty street corner for what seemed like minutes waiting for the light to change. Maybe that was why she paid more attention to her surroundings than usual, and knew after four blocks or so that someone was following her.

She knew a little about how to spot a pursuer, mostly from reading detective stories from between the two world wars. The first rush of panic came and went. Thereafter she kept her pace unchanged, and watched angled windows and auto windscreens in the hope of catching sight of her pursuer. Whoever it was apparently knew more about the art of tailing someone than she did, though. More than once she convinced herself that no one could actually be following her. Each time, though, a glance in a conveniently placed window caught a hint of motion somewhere back behind her, and she had the uncomfortable feeling between her shoulder blades that told her she was being watched.

Maybe a mugger, she thought, struggling to keep a second burst of panic at bay. Maybe a rapist. Maybe something else—and in any case she knew better than to go further east into the area between downtown and the Heydonian, where there would be even fewer pedestrians and too many places where a lone woman could be dragged out of sight. Just at that moment the street was empty of cars. She crossed to the other side midblock, went to the corner, turned, and let herself hurry just a little more down the final block to the downtown transit mall, where there were always people, usually a police officer or two, and just possibly a bus she could catch.

She was in luck. As she reached the mall, a bus came out from between two tall buildings another block away and headed for its stop close by. The sign up above the windshield had 9 LAMBSPRING POINT VIA IVY STREET on it. Ariel stifled a whoop of sheer relief and angled across the mall to the stop. She got there just as the bus opened its doors, climbed aboard and paid her fare after three other people who'd been waiting there the whole time. Once she settled in a seat behind the driver, she waited to see if anyone else boarded after her.

No one did, and she didn't see anyone obviously watching the bus as it pulled away from the curb.

The bus wound its way through the urban canyons of downtown Adocentyn, passed the old town green, and finally headed out toward the Culpeper Hill neighborhood. Ariel stayed on edge all the way from the transit mall to the corner of Lyon Avenue and Ivy Street, where she left the bus. A quick glance around didn't show anyone nearby at all, and the feeling of being watched didn't recur, but she started up the hill at the quickest pace she could manage without actually breaking into a run. Two and a half blocks later the sturdy front door of her grandfather's house shut firmly behind her. She fastened the deadbolt, let out a ragged sigh, and let herself start to feel safe again.

Once her coat was draped over the coat tree and she'd changed into baggy sweats, she got a cup of tea and settled on the parlor sofa. The grandfather clock chimed some astrological tipping point she hadn't learned yet and the beady eyes of the little wooden crocodile gazed down from its bookshelf perch. Those were comforting, and the familiar sounds of the old house were even more so. After a moment and a couple of sips of tea, she pulled the novel by Leonora Blake out of her shoulder bag, set it on the end table, and then got out the two wills and the paperwork for the sale of Leonora Blake's estate and started sorting through them.

Jasper Harshaw's will took most of the time she spent on that process. He'd left a dizzying assortment of bequests to family members, business associates, and charities, the Heydonian among them, interspersing the bequests with comments by turns wry and irritable. Exactly what his daughter Holly had done to offend him wasn't mentioned in the will, but he'd left her the house on Ithuriel Place, stipulated that none of his personal possessions were to go to her, and inserted a brusque paragraph afterward calling her a disgrace to the family and telling his other heirs not to waste a penny or a minute on her.

Ariel shook her head, kept reading, and finally found a listing for the bronze plaque with the carnelian disk, one of a dozen antiquities he'd left to his son Clarence.

Leonora Blake's will was much shorter. Her heirs were a few younger relatives in the Blake and Cray families, Theophilus Cray among them, and she didn't include comments on the bequests or their recipients, just items and names. The plaque was mentioned most of the way toward the end: *my antique Italic votive plaque with two wolves and a red moon upon it.* Along with several other items, she had intended it to go to Flavia Cray, a cousin of hers.

The records of the estate sale told a different story. Close to half of the things named in Leonora's will had been bought by Jasper Harshaw at high prices; Ariel guessed that there must have been fierce bidding. Two dozen books and a small marble statue, not otherwise described, had been purchased by Theophilus Cray, and the rest had been scattered among a handful of other relatives and collectors.

She copied down the details, feeling pleased with herself, and then went on to her shorthand. Once that was done, she picked up the novel by Leonora Blake. The title page was no more informative than such things ever are. She paged forward to the beginning of the first chapter, and found a lively opening scene waiting for her. Two women sat in a second-class saloon aboard an ocean liner in the 1930s, somewhere in the middle of the Atlantic, with tarot cards spread on the table between them. The younger woman, thirty-something and feeling it, was on her way to southern France to flee from the aftermath of a failed love affair; the older woman was interpreting the cards. From there, the story spun on agreeably, and Ariel got herself comfortably curled up and let herself sink into the novel.

She had just finished the first chapter when the front door rattled and her grandfather came back from the Heydonian. Once he'd settled in his usual chair with a cup of tea ready to hand, he asked her how her errand of the morning had gone, and listened to her account of the wills and the sale report with fingers steepled and eyes half closed.

"Very capably done," he said then, making her blush. "I'll get the details written up this afternoon, before Theophilus comes over, and present it to the board tomorrow, along with both wills and the sale record. It'll be months yet before Harshaw's estate is settled, but at this point I think the provenance is clear enough that we can justify making an offer on the plaque."

Ariel considered that. "Are all museums that careful?"

"In a perfect world, they would be." A fractional shrug dismissed the thought. "In the world we live in, quite a few museums are happy to buy a forgery if it looks convincing, and at least as many will take stolen property if they think they can do it and not be caught. The Heydonian is more ethical than some." He drank tea, considered the book on the arm of the sofa. "One of Leonora's novels?"

Ariel nodded. "*The Chapel of the Grail.* They had it at the library downtown."

"I'd be interested to know what you think of it."

"I've just finished the first chapter, but so far it's good. Weird, but good."

He allowed a fractional smile. "That's quite a good description of Leonora." Another sip finished the tea. He unfolded himself from his chair, got the wills and the estate sale papers from Ariel, and vanished into his study, from which the clatter of a keyboard came shortly after.

Another hour or so passed: enough time for Ariel to review her notes on the last week or so of Aunt Clarice's instruction, copy the essentials down in a less messy form, and take the notebooks up to her room along with Leonora Blake's novel. She was coming back down the stairs when the doorbell rang, announcing the arrival of their guest.

Theophilus Cray was no taller than Ariel and not much more heavily built. He shed a billowing coat of heavy gray wool and hung it on the coat tree in the entry; under that, he wore a white shirt with cufflinks, a red and black embroidered vest of Central Asian cut, and gray woolen slacks. Flyaway white hair, held inadequately in check by a flat-topped red cap that matched the vest, framed a wrinkled face tanned by wind and sun. He beamed at Ariel as she welcomed him in, made a deep and florid bow, and followed her into the parlor.

"Tea? By all means," he said in response to Dr. Moravec's inevitable question. One spidery hand extracted a packet from somewhere inside his vest. "Perhaps you'd like to give this a try. A very pleasant blend from Samarkand."

Dr. Moravec took it and vanished into the kitchen. Ariel said the usual things, and Cray smiled and settled on a convenient chair. "Well, my Jumbly Girl," he said, "I trust you're still enjoying life in Adocentyn."

She nodded enthusiastically. "I wouldn't move back to Summerfield for anything."

"I spent far too much time there once. Granted, it was just over fourteen minutes, but that was still far too long." He shuddered in remembered dismay. Ariel laughed, and he beamed at her and nodded, as though her laughter had proved something or other.

Dr. Moravec came back out then with an oddly shaped teapot of glazed blue ceramic and three mismatched cups. The next few minutes went into filling and distributing the cups and talk about the tea, which had a long name Ariel was sure she'd never be able to pronounce. She sipped it, decided she liked the flavor.

"Before we proceed," Dr. Moravec said then, "we should settle a few practical details. I took the liberty of reserving a table at Trattoria Udine for dinner in an hour."

"Thank you. Yes, that will be very welcome indeed."

"I'm pleased to hear it. Before then, Ariel had certain questions about photography, which I suspect she's too polite to have mentioned yet. She intends to buy a camera. Under the circumstances I thought it would be wise to bring that up now."

"Oh, very probably, yes." Cray turned to Ariel. "Photography? Is it too much to hope that you're considering genuine film photography, and not the electronic counterfeit?" She nodded, and he executed a seated bow that would have done credit to a royal court. "Yes, I can certainly advise you on that, as it's been an interest of mine for a very long time. You require suggestions on where to start? Detailed instructions?" He started to quote in a high singsong voice: "'The thing can be done,' said the butcher, 'I think. The thing must be done, that is sure. The thing shall be done! Bring me paper and ink, the best there is time to procure!'"

Ariel recognized the quote before Cray had gotten past the first sentence, and grinned: *The Hunting of the Snark* was an old favorite of hers. "I can certainly bring paper, portfolio, pens, and ink in unfailing supplies," she said, "but we're all out of strange creepy creatures." Then, remembering her experience earlier: "Well, one followed me downtown for a while this morning, I think, but I managed to lose it."

That got her the sudden attention of both of them. "You didn't mention this," said Dr. Moravec. "Perhaps you can describe what happened."

"Sure," said Ariel, with an uncertain glance at him and then at Cray. She explained the events of the morning, the sense of someone watching her, the presence faintly glimpsed in angled windows, the bus that had provided her with a means of escape.

Once she was done, Cray gave her grandfather a sharp glance and said, "You haven't taught her tradecraft yet? You'll forgive me, Bernard, but that seems a little unwise."

"Her current studies," said Dr. Moravec, "include an apprenticeship with Clarice Jackson, two sessions of scrying practice daily, and Gregg system shorthand. That seemed like a tolerably full schedule for the time being."

"What's tradecraft?" Ariel asked.

"The practical side of espionage," Dr. Moravec said. "The art of surveillance belongs to tradecraft, and also the art of avoiding surveillance." He allowed a fractional shrug. "I learned a certain amount of it when I worked for the government. In those days Washington was crawling with Eastern Bloc agents and everyone at the agency from top executives to night janitors had to be on the alert constantly. As an intelligence analyst, I was no exception. Since then, I've put the same skills to work tolerably often in investigations."

"I think," said Cray, "that an introductory lesson sometime soon might be worth your while, my Jumbly Girl. A lesson, that is, in how to detect and avoid pursuit. I would be entirely willing to provide it. Two hours, perhaps, then a trip to a camera store and lunch? I can promise you that it will at the very least be entertaining."

Ariel considered that and said, "I bet. Sure, let's do it."

Chapter 7

A FLEETING IMAGE

The following Saturday was the first day she and Cray both had free. He'd explained over salad at Trattoria Udine that his way of teaching tradecraft was entirely practical. She was to walk someplace, he would follow, and she would try to shake him loose and get some experience in how to deal with pursuit. He beamed as he said it, and Ariel wondered just how good he was at tradecraft and where he'd learned it.

Over the next few days, she spent more than one hour leafing through the pages of old detective novels she owned. Dashiell Hammett had actually been a private investigator, she thought she recalled, but she wasn't sure whether she could use anything Raymond Chandler and Dorothy Sayers had written on the subject. Did they really know about detective work, or were they just making it all up? She could not tell. Still, on Friday night she put a few extra things into the floppy blue shoulder bag she meant to carry for her tradecraft lesson.

The next morning dawned clear and cold. Her scrying practice was no more productive than usual, and she had to struggle to stay focused as she went through the morning paper—it was one of her chores to read it and clip any stories her grandfather might find useful. Finally, though, she picked up a manila envelope full of photocopies her grandfather had asked her to drop off at the Heydonian's front office, donned an inconspicuous brown coat, shouldered the bulky blue bag, and headed out the door.

Even though she knew Cray wouldn't be following her yet, her nerves were on edge as she walked the familiar route to the Heydonian. Cars drove past, and it occurred to her suddenly that the people in any one of them might be watching her. Now and again someone walked past her. Was it an innocent pedestrian, or something more sinister? She couldn't be sure. She found that she was watching everyone and everything around her.

It occurred to her as the first glimpse of the Heydonian's white marble dome came into sight ahead of her that she'd managed to stumble into the "situational awareness" Cray had talked about at the restaurant. That pleased her, but it also made her wonder what it would be like to pay that kind of attention to everything whenever she set foot outside. Another thought followed a moment later: wasn't that what Sherlock Holmes did every moment of his life? She thought about that the rest of the way to the Heydonian.

Her footfalls echoed off the ceiling of the big entrance hall as she went to the door to the office, halfway along the wall with the portraits. She was almost there when the door opened and someone came out of it, a bland balding little man in a heavy black woolen coat. He glanced at her; brown eyes circled by round-framed glasses registered her existence, blinked as if uncertain, looked elsewhere. He held the door open for her. Once she'd thanked him, he turned and hurried away toward the front entrance. Only as she entered the office did Ariel realize that she'd seen him before at the county courthouse.

She handed over the manila envelope to Marjorie Quiller, the Heydonian Institution's secretary, exchanged a few polite words and then went back out into the hall. From there she went to an elevator she'd never approached before. It was on the left side of the entrance hall, in a little alcove not far from the double glass doors that led into the Heydonian Museum.

It had only one button on the panel beside it, and that lacked an arrow pointing either up or down. Instead, a loudspeaker grill pierced the metal plate just above the button, and a horizontal slot not otherwise marked gaped open just below it.

She pushed the button. After a moment, a male voice, old and hard as flint, said, "Yes?"

"I was told to call for Mr. Cray," said Ariel.

"I'll tell him," said the voice.

At that instant, the elevator doors slid open to reveal Theophilus Cray in a long gray coat and a floppy wool hat. Ariel did a doubletake and then started laughing. Cray beamed, executed an ornate bow, and said, "Good morning, my Jumbly Girl! Ready for today's adventure?"

"Probably not," Ariel admitted. "But I'll do my best."

"That's the spirit." He left the elevator, motioned toward the entrance. The two of them walked to the doors. "So," said Cray. "Do you remember what I told you at Trattoria Udine?"

"I think so."

"Good. I'll give you—" He extracted a pocket watch on a chain from inside his coat. "Five minutes precisely to make a start. After that, I'll follow you like a hound. If you make any highly predictable moves, expect to find me waiting for you."

"The way you were waiting in the elevator?" said Ariel, and when he beamed again and nodded: "How did you do that?"

"Oh, that. I waited by a window upstairs until I saw you on the sidewalk, took the elevator down to the main floor, used the button that holds the doors closed, and waited until I heard your voice. A simple trick. I may be using some that are less simple today."

She gave him an uncertain look, but he smiled and said nothing more. A moment later they reached the doors. "Five minutes!" he said, and motioned for her to go.

By the time she was on the sidewalk she'd made her first decisions. They'd agreed to meet at the camera store on Flagler Way, but she knew better than to go in that direction at once.

Instead, she went the opposite direction, and turned onto a narrow side street as quickly as she could. Another block, and a glance in a convenient windshield showed her what she expected to see: a hint of gray well behind her, letting her know that Cray was on her track.

She sped up a little, turned the next corner, and spotted a business she knew on the other side of the street, a pleasant little breakfast-and-lunch café. She'd been in it once before, and—yes, it had a door in back, opening onto an alley and the parking lot beyond. A momentary break in the traffic got her across the street. She went in the front door of the café, hurried through a narrow room with a few patrons sipping coffee at tables, darted down the hallway behind past restroom doors and went out the door into the alley.

Cray was waiting for her in the parking lot. He beamed, and motioned for her to go. Reddening, she turned down the alley, rounded the corner onto a narrow cross street. A glance behind showed her that he hadn't started following her yet. She put on speed, went back around to the front door of the café, ducked back into it again, went straight back to the restrooms, and extracted her secret weapons from the blue shoulder bag.

A moment later, dressed in a dull red coat and a knit woolen hat and carrying a well-filled brown shoulder bag, she went out the back entrance and turned the other direction down the alley. Cray wasn't in sight this time. She made herself walk slowly, as though she had nothing to worry about and no one could possibly be following her. A block passed, another, and then she left the alley and went along another narrow street that angled more or less toward the camera shop down on Flagler Way. The streets downtown had begun to fill up with pedestrians, and she tried to match their pace and do nothing to call attention to herself.

She didn't expect to get away from Cray's experienced gaze for long, and after another block she felt a prickle between her shoulder blades. Did that mean she was being watched, or just that her nerves were too much on edge? She knew better than to guess. The street had enough pedestrians in it by then that she couldn't be sure she was being followed, but windows and windshields gave her a few glimpses of someone going the same way she was who seemed to be matching her pace. He wore a dark coat, not the gray coat Cray had been wearing. The thought that both of them had used the same trick made her grin.

She wasn't out of options yet, though. Up ahead she spotted a shopping arcade full of little stores, a place she'd visited a few times since her move to Adocentyn. It filled half of a block and had five doors on three streets; even more to the point, it contained plenty of places to hide. In she went at the first door she reached, and scurried into the second store on the left, a narrow little space that sold odd trinkets and cheap antiques. From the back corner of the shop, the corridor out in front was half hidden by an artificial Christmas tree decked with ornaments for sale. Ariel got behind that, watched the corridor, and waited. The store clerk gave her an incurious glance and then went back to doing something on his phone. In the corridor, a dozen people drifted by. Then, to her delight, Theophilus Cray went past.

His pace looked leisurely, and he glanced from side to side with a mild expression on his face, as though he was shopping for holiday presents. He was wearing his gray coat again. Clever, Ariel thought, and waited. He didn't seem to notice her. Once he was past, she moved gradually up to the front of the store. There he was, still moving away from her, his hat just visible among the other shoppers. That was all she needed; she hurried out the doors and went a block back the way she'd come, then got off the street as quickly as she could and dodged two blocks toward the old waterfront before turning south toward the camera store again.

That time she reached Flagler Way before she thought she caught a glimpse of someone following her. It was impossible to be sure, since there were plenty of pedestrians by then, but the way Cray had been waiting for her behind the café still smarted. She was still three blocks from the camera store, and decided to try one more evasive maneuver before she got there. A big brick Victorian building with commercial spaces on the ground floor and CASPERSON BUILDING carved into its cornice offered the opportunity she needed. She'd been there before, too, and knew that the shops on the ground floor had doors onto a big open stairwell in the middle of the building, one that went all the way up to skylights six stories above.

That was workable, she decided. She went into the first available shop, which was a bookstore. It wasn't the kind of bookstore she usually visited. It was full of the latest fashionable novels and an assortment of political books with angry titles, and the children's section in back was far too well stocked with Bertie Scrubb novels for her taste—that popular and lucrative series, with its parade of fake wizardry, had already begun to annoy her even before she'd started to learn about magic, and the bookstore display was overstocked with one of the more popular spinoffs from the series, a heavily illustrated volume about three magic ponies who turned into boys. Ariel curled her lip, but spent a minute or so strolling through the shop and pretending to look at the bookshelves before ducking through the door in back into the stairwell.

A quick glance around spotted no convenient hiding places on that floor. Moving as quickly and quietly as she could, she went up the stair to the next floor, and found a place on the floor above where she had a decent view of the doors below and could get out of sight into a poorly lit corner with a few fast steps. She waited. Minutes passed, and nothing happened. Then the back door of the bookshop opened and someone glanced out. Cray, she guessed, though she couldn't see enough of him to be sure and she wasn't willing to risk being spotted.

Whoever it was, he was gone an instant later. Ariel waited, guessed that Cray was gone, and started for the stair. Halfway there she stopped, and changed back into her brown coat and blue shoulder bag. Then, trying to suppress a grin, she went back down the stair, spotted a sign marked EXIT, and a minute later was on the next street. Two blocks toward downtown and a block up a cross street brought her to Flagler Way, two doors from Bill's Camera. A quick glance around showed no visible sign of Cray. Moments later she was in front of the camera store.

The door creaked a little as she opened it. Inside, a waist-high glass case that doubled as a counter ran along one side, with just enough space behind it for the proprietor. A lobby not that much wider, with two chairs and an umbrella stand in it, filled the other side back to a door labeled PRIVATE. The glass case was full of cameras, and the wall behind had a mix of brightly colored posters from camera manufacturers and elegant framed black and white photos of ships and beach scenes.

Most of Ariel's attention, though, went to the two people in the store. Behind the counter was a plump little man in jeans and a green cotton shirt, with a round face and a shock of white hair. In front was a woman in her thirties who wore a knee-length bright red leather jacket cut tight to show her curves. She had ash-blonde highlights in her brown hair and a taut hard look on her face, and she leaned forward with both hands on the counter as though she meant to bite the plump man's head off and swallow it in one gulp.

"I want you to fix it," she hissed.

The plump man shrugged. "Nothing I can do. The film's fine, the camera's fine, the image ain't on the negatives."

"But it was *there!*"

He shrugged again, palms up. "Not on the negatives it wasn't. You can take the film to another place, they'll tell you the same thing."

The woman snatched up something on the counter—a stack of photos, Ariel guessed—and stuffed it into her red leather purse. "On the other hand, maybe they'll be competent.

Unlike you." She turned away, livid, and saw Ariel standing just inside the door. "Don't bother with this stupid shop," she snarled. "You'll just waste your money." She stalked out, making Ariel flatten herself against the wall to keep from being shoved aside.

The door slammed. Ariel glanced after her, looked back at the man behind the counter, who met her gaze with a tentative smile.

"I hope you don't get a lot of customers like that," said Ariel.

The man's smile became a little less forced. "It happens. What can I do for you? The name's Bill, in case the sign outside didn't tell you. Bill Kotzebue."

Ariel went over to the counter. "Pleased to meet you." Since Cray was still nowhere to be seen, she went on. "I'm Ariel Moravec, and I'm looking for a beginner's camera, not too expensive. I want to get started in film photography."

He brightened visibly. "Okay, fair enough. Ever used a camera?"

"Just the one in my cell phone."

"Got it. Looking at 35 millimeter?" When she nodded: "Good. These days, even with film starting to come back into fashion, that's the one size you can always count on getting. What kind of photography do you have in mind?"

"I don't know yet," Ariel admitted. "I want to try different things."

"Smart. Okay, you might want to take a look at this." He opened the back of the glass case, got out a camera. "Your basic point and shoot beginner's camera. It's better than twice as old as you are, but it's in really good condition, and you don't get that quality new these days without paying through the nose." Ariel took it from him, considered it, and glanced at the price tag: it was only a little over half of what she'd budgeted for the purchase. She raised it, looked through the viewfinder at nothing in particular.

"That would be a fine choice," said Theophilus Cray behind her.

Startled, she glanced back. There he was, comfortably settled in one of the chairs as though he'd been there all along, though she hadn't heard the door open.

"Mr. Cray!" said Bill. "Good to see you."

"Likewise," said Cray. "Oh, please carry on, Bill. I'll be buying some film shortly, but I'm in no hurry."

Ariel turned back to the camera. It was a plain Japanese model with a built-in flash. It didn't have f-stops marked on the lens barrel or a shutter speed dial on top, but she'd resigned herself to upgrading later on to something that old-fashioned, once she'd learned the basics.

"Let's see," said Bill, delving into the lower reaches of the glass case. "Okay, good. I've got the case and the owner's manual for that one, too. Of course everything I sell comes with a warranty. I've got a lady who does repairs, she's absolutely first-rate."

Ariel nodded, deciding. "This looks really good," she said. "I'll take it."

"Sold," Bill said, grinning. "While we're at it, I hope I can interest you in some film."

Over the next ten minutes Ariel bought the camera and twelve rolls of film, half of them color and the rest black and white. She took in a quick informal lesson on how to load the film and use the camera, and got treated to a good-sized helping of Bill Kotzebue's enthusiasm for all things photographic. "I do my own developing," he told her as he rang up the purchase. "You got labs going back into the business again, just like old times, but I've still got the developing machine my dad bought when he got this store started back in '75, and it purrs like a furry little kitten. I beat anybody else's price, too."

The camera in its padded case went into Ariel's shoulder bag, finding a place next to the spare coat and the other shoulder bag, and so did a paper bag with the film in it. When Ariel thanked him, he grinned and said, "Hey, I ought to thank you. After that last customer, I really needed someone who knows how to be nice."

Ariel blushed. "What was her problem?"

He rolled his eyes. "She was doing night shots up by Culpeper Park, good quality black and white film, thought she had all her ducks in a row, okay? This dog comes along and she snaps a bunch of pictures of it. I develop the film, and there's the trees, the sidewalk—" He shrugged. "No dog. Mistook a shadow for a dog, or maybe she was smoking a little too much of that wacky tobaccy." Ariel choked, and he grinned again. "Lots of photographers are nice people, but you get some like her. Really makes you wonder." He turned. "Now you wanted some film, Mr. Cray. What can I get you?"

They got that settled promptly, and Cray found a place inside his long gray coat for a paper bag with two dozen rolls of exotic film in it. A few pleasantries later, he and Ariel stepped back out onto the sidewalk. "So how did I do?" Ariel asked him.

"For a beginner, quite tolerably well." He gestured to the crosswalk nearby. "Shall we proceed to lunch? It's been an interesting morning—more interesting than I expected, in fact. We can discuss that once we're comfortable."

Five minutes, maybe, found the two of them on Moon Street, a little more than a block past Aunt Clarice's shop. "Here we are," said Cray, motioning toward a metal-framed glass door. The sign above it, a slab of dark wood, had four ornate Japanese characters, a stylized flower, and the words OHANA NOODLE BAR carved into it and painted in faded gold. Inside, scroll paintings hung on sagging plaster walls, little tables with dark blue tablecloths ran along one wall, and a bar with tall bar stools ran along the other. Hissing sounds from somewhere further back spoke of a grill in use, half drowning out music from loudspeakers overhead: a melody in a scale

Ariel didn't recognize, played on a plucked string instrument she didn't recognize either.

As the door swung shut an old woman in a blue and white happi coat came out from behind the bar, smiling. She bowed to Cray, who bowed back. Her name was Mrs. Kishida; Cray introduced Ariel to her; they spoke in Japanese for a little while, and then Mrs. Kishida led them to a table at the very back of the establishment, next to the hallway that led back to the restrooms. Cray waved Ariel to a chair and sat facing the window out front.

Tea, menus, and steamed soybeans in the pod made a prompt appearance. "This is the cat's pajamas," said Ariel. "I didn't even know it was here."

"Moon Street has some remarkable little shops and restaurants on it," Cray said. "Not all of them advertise themselves. Very convenient for certain things."

Ariel wondered what those things were, decided that a different question came first. "You said that the morning was more interesting than you expected. What happened?"

"It's quite simple, really. We chose an unusually good time for a lesson in tradecraft, because I wasn't the only one who was following you this morning."

Chapter 8

A GAME PLAYED FOR BLOOD

Appalled, Ariel considered him for a moment, then swallowed and said, "Okay."

"I spotted your other pursuer a few minutes after we met out behind the café," Cray went on. "He's quite competent, and he seems to have noticed me about the same time I noticed him. He didn't want me to see him, though of course he wanted to know who I was. I had the same goals. So we followed you and dodged each other. I didn't get a clear look at him at any point, and I don't believe he got a clear look at me."

"I wonder what he was after," said Ariel.

"Oh, he wanted to find out where you were going and why. One thing you'll learn very quickly is the difference between the pursuer who wants to catch up to you and the pursuer who wants to keep his distance. This one kept his distance, so you were in no physical danger."

She nodded, sipped tea to cover her discomfiture.

"That went on until you went out the back of the Casperson Building."

"So you figured that out," said Ariel, feeling deflated.

"Only once I located you again, and I don't believe your other pursuer found you any sooner than I did. He kept his distance after that point. He seems to have decided that you knew you were being followed, and—" A shrug punctuated the sentence. "For a beginner, as I said, you did quite tolerably well. I didn't expect the red coat and the hat, for example—where did you learn that trick?"

She blushed. "From a Lord Peter Wimsey mystery."

"*Have His Carcase*, I imagine? Good. Very good. Dorothy Sayers was the best English mystery writer of her generation. Why Agatha Christie has the reputation she does, I have no idea." He shuddered visibly.

Just then Mrs. Kishida came back to refill their teacups and take their orders. Once she was gone, Cray went on. "That maneuver threw my rival off your track, for a little while. Myself, I've made a habit of watching gaits. Do you realize that how a person walks is as distinctive as a fingerprint? Yes, it's quite remarkable. Of course you also didn't change your shoes, and so that clinched the matter."

Ariel glanced down at her shoes, and then laughed. "Okay, got it. I've got a lot to learn."

"Of course. You're learning the rules of a game that has been played for blood since long before the time of Agharta."

She glanced up at him from the bowl of soybeans, startled; she'd already learned that the name of the lost city of the central Asian deserts wasn't something to mention lightly. His face showed no trace of his usual levity. "Is it okay," she said, "if I ask how you learned this stuff?"

"Oh, you can always ask." A smile crept back into its usual place. "I might even tell you the answer someday."

She considered him, and sipped tea.

Their orders came a moment later, accompanied by chopsticks and Western silverware. Ariel wasn't confident enough with chopsticks to risk trying to eat her noodle dish with them, but it didn't surprise her at all that Cray picked up his pair and used them with the deftness of long practice. He changed the subject just as deftly, giving her half a dozen pieces of advice on how to throw off someone following her, and then veered suddenly into a story about her grandfather. As lunch wound down and he finished up the narrative, she caught a familiar name.

"My grandfather's told me a little about Leonora Blake," she said then. "He said you introduced him to her."

"I did indeed." He gestured with his chopsticks. "Bernard was quite the little lost lamb when he first came here." Ariel choked with laughter, and Cray waggled a finger at her. "No, you must never suppress a laugh. It's shockingly bad for your health. Let me see—yes, this was in 1992. Bernard and I had been in contact for a good long while by then, since not long after his divorce, in fact. He came up to visit now and then, but he knew nobody but me when he arrived, and he's not the type who makes friends readily if he's left to himself. So I took him to a pleasant little café for lunch with Aunt Leonora, and they hit it off well from the first.

"But that friendship eased his way into certain circles at the Heydonian, and Bernard also had the supreme good sense to make the acquaintance of Marjorie Williams—you might have heard of her: Aunt Clarice Jackson's grandmother. She was far and away the best diviner in Adocentyn in her day. Back then some of the old families around the Heydonian wouldn't so much as speak to her because of her race. Bernard, being a sensible man, ignored all of that nonsense. He visited her for weekly readings as long as she lived."

"He goes to Aunt Clarice for a reading every Tuesday now," said Ariel.

"Oh, I know. He's benefited a great deal from that, and not just because of the readings. The politics of the Heydonian are complex, my Jumbly Girl, and so are the politics of this city. Doubtless you'll have to deal with those in due time, but I won't darken your day by recounting them. We have something else to be concerned about."

She glanced up from the last of her noodles. "Oh?"

"It's quite possible that your other pursuer is waiting somewhere outside. I haven't seen him from here, but he's competent enough that I wouldn't."

Ariel wrestled down a sudden burst of panic. "What should I do?"

"Good. Very good. Yes, the practical question is the one to consider first. What you should do, if you're willing, is to finish up this very pleasant meal as though nothing could possibly be wrong. In a minute or so I'll go back to the restroom, or that will be the appearance of it. A few minutes after that, you'll pay for the meal—" He extracted some bills from a pocket, placed them on the table. "Then you'll leave, as though you haven't the least concern in the world. You'll go somewhere downtown not too far away, following a route we'll arrange in advance. If anyone follows you, I'll be aware of it, and I'll confront him."

She gave him a dubious look. "Do you think that's safe?"

"For me? Entirely. For your pursuer, possibly not." Cray chuckled. "No, my Jumbly Girl, you mustn't worry about me. You look at me and see a strange and slightly silly old man. It pleases me to be seen that way." He learned forward. In a low precise voice: "I've killed rather more men than you've seen birthdays. Never without very good reason, and generally when my own life was at stake, but the fact remains." He sat back, put on a broad smile as though shrugging on a coat. "Shall we choose a place and a route, then?"

That took only a very few words. Once that was settled, Cray got up, touched his head with one hand as though tapping the brim of a hat, and went back into the narrow hallway. Ariel made a point of not looking that way until she heard a door open and close. She finished her tea, and half turned in the chair to see if she could attract Mrs. Kishida's attention.

A few minutes later Ariel went out the front door of the Ohana Noodle Bar onto Moon Street, and started toward downtown. Her nerves were keyed up, her senses straining, but if anyone followed her she didn't see or sense any trace of that fact. Moon Street yielded to Flagler Way, half-familiar buildings gave way to the old town green with Elias Ashmole's statue in its usual place, and that gave way in turn to older buildings she knew slightly better, and to her goal.

The faded words on the sign up above the door read DUPOIS & CO. ANTIQUE BOOKSELLERS. Ariel looked up at them, then looked at the oval window in the middle of the door. The space inside seemed dark and empty, but the iron bars that blocked the doorway during the store's off hours had been folded out to the sides and a demure little sign in black and white hung in the middle of the oval, bearing the one word OPEN. She went forward and tried the knob. The door swung open, setting a little bell chiming, and let her into the bookshop.

The few times she'd visited Dupois & Company before then, the shop's one big room had been so crammed with books she'd wondered why there were none stacked on the blades of the ceiling fans. She looked around and saw that things hadn't changed worth noticing. A pink-faced, rotund man in beige slacks and a brown jacket, with a gold silk ascot showing at his throat and a fringe of silver hair showing just above his ears, glanced her way, noted her existence, found it uninteresting, and returned to a book he was considering. A lean old black woman in a vivid yellow coat looked up from a table covered with books, smiled, and turned back to the table. Other than those two people, the ceiling, and narrow paths crossing the floor, books filled her entire field of view: rank upon rank of them in bookcases that rose from floor to ceiling, heaps of them on tables, stacks of them here and there on the floor.

It occurred to Ariel a moment after the door closed behind her that she had no idea what she was supposed to do in the bookstore, other than wait for Theophilus Cray to put in an appearance. A plausible excuse occurred to her a moment later. If any bookshop in Adocentyn had Leonora Blake's books, she knew it would be Dupois & Company. A glance around brought up the obvious difficulty: finding anything at all in that wilderness of books made a needle in a haystack sound easy.

Fortunately a head topped with brown hair poked out from between two of the shelves further back just then. A moment later the rest of the clerk emerged and came toward her: a thin young man in a forest green sweater and gray woolen slacks. A single bushy eyebrow crossed from one side of his face to the other without a break in the middle; below that, blue eyes regarded her over the top of a pair of narrow reading glasses. Ariel, who had spoken to him briefly two months before, tried to recall his name and failed.

"Good afternoon," he said. "What can I do for you?"

"I'm looking for books by Leonora Blake," said Ariel. "Her novels or her poetry. I don't know where to look for them, though."

That earned her a faint upward movement of the eyebrow. "If we have anything it'll be over here." He turned around and headed back; a motion of his head signaled her to follow.

The narrow path he traced between tables and stacks of books went most of the way to the back of the store. There, one series of shelves had small pieces of card taped to them, reading FICTION BY AUTHOR. "Any of her novels we've got in stock ought to be here," he said. "Poetry's over there—" A gesture indicated another set of shelves marked with a card saying POETRY BY AUTHOR. "We had some books by her out of an estate sale, but I don't know if we've still got them. Are you a fan of hers?"

"Well, kind of," said Ariel. "I read one of her novels and liked it."

He nodded. "Strange old lady. I never met her but my grandma told me some really odd stories about her." She gave him a startled look, but by then he was already turning away. She watched him head back to whatever he had been doing in among the stacks, then turned to the shelves in front of her and began to hunt.

Ten minutes passed without success, partly because the words BY AUTHOR on the little handwritten signs turned out to be wishful thinking at best, and partly because she only knew one title of Leonora Blake's and so had to check anything that didn't have an author's name on the spine. A gray clothbound volume long since deprived of its dust jacket rewarded her eventually; it had *Pilgrimage to Montségur—Blake* on the spine, and turned out to be a copy of Blake's first novel, in respectable condition and not too expensive. That encouraged her to keep hunting. Further down, near the bottom of the shelf, she found a copy of *The Chapel of the Grail* that could have been the twin of the one she'd found in the library, except that it had the original dust jacket on it. It wasn't overpriced, either, and she recalled how little she'd spent on the camera and decided to get them both.

She was searching the bottom shelf of the fiction section, just above floor level, when Theophilus Cray appeared. The door chimed open, though she couldn't see it from where she was crouching. Not long after, Cray came back through the store as though he knew exactly where to find her. "Good afternoon, my Jumbly Girl," he said, bowing, as she scrambled to her feet. "I'm sorry to say that our mutual friend must have had pressing business elsewhere. He was nowhere to be seen."

Ariel grinned with relief and got to her feet. "Well, I'm not too upset."

"Understandably. Still, it would have been helpful to know who it was." He extracted a business card from inside his coat. "With today's practice under your belt, you should have a somewhat easier time evading anyone who follows you. We can discuss more advanced methods of evasion if that becomes necessary, of course. In the meantime, if you're followed again, call me as soon as possible. Any time, night or day. Understood?"

She nodded, and he beamed at her. "Well, it has been a very pleasant and instructive few hours. I'm sorry to say that less interesting duties call me. We'll see each other soon, we'll see each other soon, we'll see each other soon."

"What you tell me three times is true?" Ariel said, laughing.

"Count on it." He bowed again, wished her a good afternoon, and left the store.

The rest of the fiction shelves brought her no further surprises. She crossed to the poetry shelves and started searching. That was considerably slower going, since most of the slender books there had nothing on their spines at all. Finally, though, when she'd nearly given up, she pulled out a thin volume bound in damp-spotted green cloth, opened it, and saw Leonora Blake's name on the title page.

That turned out to be a volume of poems titled *The Wind in the Sedges*. A glance inside showed a sonnet that looked interesting; she flipped forward to the title page and found facing it a list of other books of poetry: *Bright Were the Halls Then*, *Counsels of the Sea*, and *Cedars in Fog*. Those sounded interesting, too, and she returned to the hunt with renewed enthusiasm. That didn't change the fact that none of those, nor anything else by Leonora Blake, was waiting for her. She frowned, but added her one find to the novels, tucked the lot under one arm and headed for the sales counter in front.

At first glance she thought the clerk had gone somewhere else, and wondered whether she should go look for him, but then he stood up from behind the desk—Ariel gathered he'd been doing something with yet another pile of books. "Can I—" he started to say, then spotted the books under her arm. "Oh, good. I was hoping no one else had gotten those."

She sent a smile his way. "Thank you."

He took the books with a matching smile, set them on the desk, got out a ledger. Dupois & Co. hadn't modernized its sales system in many decades, Ariel gathered, for the title and price of every book had to be entered by hand in the ledger, and then the total added up on a paper receipt pad. While the clerk was busy with that, Ariel considered him, and also what he'd said earlier. "I wonder," she said when he was almost finished, "if you'd be willing to tell me the stories you heard from your grandmother."

He glanced up at her from the receipt pad. "About Leonora Blake? Sure." He tipped his head to one side. "Maybe I can buy you a cup of coffee sometime."

Ariel considered that and decided she was up for it. "You're on," she said, and reached into her purse for the spiral-bound notepad where she kept her schedule. A little more conversation settled the details: Monday at four at Seven Stars, a little coffee place across from the transit mall downtown, which Ariel had seen but never visited.

When she left the store she was feeling unexpectedly cheerful, but the thought that her second pursuer might be watching her from the shadows put a damper on that. She considered making a beeline for the transit mall, decided instead to put some of the day's lessons to work and took a roundabout route there. If anyone followed her she caught no trace of it. The bus home came promptly enough, and the ride back to the Culpeper Hill neighborhood and the three-block walk to her grandfather's house went without incident.

The rest of the afternoon and evening were no more memorable. Only two things worth noting happened during those hours, and she didn't realize their significance until later. The first happened when she spent a little while considering her new books before putting them into the bookshelf in her bedroom. That was when she read the copy on the inside back cover flap of the dust jacket of *The Chapel of the Grail*, and discovered the title of Leonora Blake's other novel: *The Carnelian Moon*. That intrigued her. Was it about the bronze plaque with the wolves? She made a note to look for a copy, and put the books away.

The other thing worth noting didn't happen until she was getting ready for bed that night. Her practice with the shewstone went a little more smoothly than usual, and for once she managed the trick of noticing the vague blurring in the center of the crystal ball without letting it distract her or make her lose her focus. It thickened and turned into something like thick mist, and then something came through it: a wolf, lean and gray and shaggy. It seemed to be stalking something, though she couldn't tell what.

An instant later the image was gone. Ariel blinked, finished up the rest of the five minutes, and wrote up the details of the practice in her notebook. The books she was studying told her to treat any image that appeared in the crystal like a dream that needed to be interpreted, but she was too sleepy by then to put much effort into making sense of the wolf. She got into bed, curled up around Nicodemus, and slipped into murky dreams where she spent some of the night searching through old unfamiliar rooms for something she couldn't remember, and some of it being hunted by something she couldn't see.

CHAPTER 9

ECHOES OF AN OLDER WORLD

"Up for another movie?" Cassie asked toward the end of the day on Monday, when the two of them were elbow deep in herbs.

"Sure," said Ariel, then caught herself. "Well, depends on the movie. What is it?"

"*Breakfast at Tiffany's.*" Cassie looked smug. "Romantic comedy from 1961. Audrey Hepburn, George Peppard, Mickey Rooney, and a cat named Cat. I forget which really famous song Hepburn sings. The Apollo's running it Friday night."

"That sounds darb," Ariel said. Cassie's expression showed clearly enough that she didn't remember what "darb" meant but didn't want to admit it, and Ariel went on: "Let's do it. Are Orion and Danny interested?"

"Oh, Orion'll be there for the music. Danny? Probably not, but we'll see."

Ariel brushed herb dust off her hands, got into her purse and wrote down the details in one of her notebooks.

Just under an hour later she and Cassie said their goodbyes to Aunt Clarice and each other and spilled out the door onto Moon Street. From there Ariel headed downtown along the same route she'd taken from the Ohana Noodle Bar two days before. She'd stepped out the front door of Aunt Clarice's shop in a distracted state, her mind full of stray thoughts, but once she was alone on the sidewalk, something of the state of awareness she'd practiced while trying to evade Theophilus Cray came back instantly. It unnerved her a little to notice every other person on the street, every car that went by, every movement within sight, but she reminded herself again that Sherlock Holmes spent every minute in that state of mind.

What would it be like to live that way? The thought hovered, unanswerable.

She got to the Seven Stars coffee shop at a few minutes to four, and relaxed a little when she glanced in the window. It wasn't the kind of coffee place she disliked, a corporate franchise where everything was bright and polished and soulless. Instead, it had secondhand tables of varying shapes and sizes, tablecloths that were clean but noticeably shabby, oil paintings in ornate frames on the walls and equally ornate light fixtures overhead. She could only see a few of the customers through the windows, but none of them seemed to be paying attention to her as she came to the door.

Once Ariel got inside she spotted the clerk from Dupois & Company easily enough. He was sitting at a table toward the back of the shop, doing something with his hands that she couldn't see. He looked up as soon as she came through the door, came to meet her, said hello a little awkwardly, bought her a coffee and raised his single eyebrow a little when she ordered a plain Americano with cream and sugar. Those preliminaries taken care of and the usual questions asked and answered, they settled at a slightly battered wooden table toward the back of the shop, under the brooding gaze of a portrait of an old man in medieval armor.

It was only after she'd sat down that she saw what he'd been doing. A square of blue paper sat on the table, creased in an odd pattern. "Origami?" Ariel asked.

He smiled. "Yeah. What's your favorite kind of bird?"

"Crows," she said. "I like their attitude."

His smile broadened. "Easy peasy." Long fingers folded and twisted, and the paper turned into a crow-shape, hunched over a little as though it sat on a branch eyeing something on the ground below. "Here you are," he said, and she thanked him and tucked it in her purse.

"So your grandmother knew Leonora Blake?" she asked then.

"Yeah." He sipped at his coffee. "I haven't had the chance to ask her anything about it, because Sundays she's always off at the White Eagles ladies auxiliary meeting until all hours." He made a little choked noise in his throat. "My family."

"Complicated?" Ariel guessed.

"You have no idea. You don't even know my name." Ariel blushed, because she'd been trying to recall his name for two days with no success. Fortunately he was staring at his coffee and didn't notice. "I go by Austin Wronski because that doesn't make people giggle. The name on my driver's license is Ladislaus Augustine Wronski-Bonaparte."

Ariel managed to hold back a laugh. "Seriously? Like the French emperor?"

He glanced up at her then with a little lopsided smile. "Yeah, one of my ancestors married a second cousin of Napoleon III. She was thirty years old and had a face like the back end of a bulldog, he was a dashing young cavalry officer who'd had an arm shot off in I forget which war, it was an arranged marriage to make the emperor happy, so of course they were blissfully happy together and had three kids."

She covered her mouth with one hand, but this time the laughter leaked out anyway. "And that's what my family is like," said Austin. "I called up my mom yesterday and got her to tell me as many of Grandma's stories as she remembered. She's only a Wronski-Bonaparte by marriage so she's got some common sense."

Ariel laughed again. "Okay," she said, "I'll keep that in mind. What did she tell you?"

That got her another one of his smiles. "That is to say, cut the clowning and get on with it. You do this for a living, don't you?"

"I work for my grandfather," Ariel said. "He's a private investigator, and if you ask me what he's investigating I'm going to smile and say nothing."

"Got it." He drank more coffee. "Okay, Leonora Blake. She was some kind of relative of my dad's French cousins, so Grandma knew her socially. It wouldn't have happened otherwise because the Blakes were high society in town back then. Did you go to high school in this state?" Ariel nodded, and he went on: "Remember Endymion Blake, the Civil War cavalry general, who was in the state senate afterwards? He was her great-uncle, or something like that. Back in the day, the Blakes owned a big mansion up past where Culpeper Park is now, and a whole bunch of real estate downtown. So Leonora Blake was in Adocentyn's upper crust when she was a girl. Her family owned a lot of shares in the Heydonian, if you know about that."

Ariel nodded again. "I know Theophilus Cray."

"I thought so. I saw the two of you talking in the store on Saturday. Strange old guy." He finished his coffee, gestured at her cup. "Another?"

She glanced at the cup, realized she'd barely touched it. "Once I've finished this one."

That earned her another lopsided smile. He got up, bought another coffee, came back. "But you've probably looked all that up already. The thing Grandma said about Leonora Blake is that she was a werewolf."

Ariel gave him a startled look, but he was staring into his coffee again. "Grandma won't talk about that unless she's had too much slivovitz, so back when we were younger my cousins and me always asked her about it over the holidays. That's what she always said. Leonora was a sweet old lady who liked to go to social events, but on the night of the full moon she'd stay home and lock herself in her bedroom, because she turned into a wolf, or something like that."

"Some women," Ariel said, "have a different reason for locking themselves in their rooms once a month." She watched his face as she said that; it was a source of mild amusement to her to watch young men go squishy-faced when periods were mentioned.

To her surprise, Austin just shrugged. "Grandma didn't think it was that. Her parents came here from France right after the war, and they told her there were traditions about *loups-garous* in the part of France where they lived. That's 'werewolves' in French."

"I know," said Ariel. "I read French."

"Not a common skill these days," he said. "That coffee's going to get cold, by the way."

She blushed, sipped at it.

"Why an Americano?"

"I'm old-fashioned," Ariel admitted. "I like coffee to taste like coffee, not like some kind of hot milkshake." Glancing at him: "But you were telling me about Leonora Blake."

"Good," he said. "I can see why your grandfather hired you." He leaned forward, propping his elbows on the table and his chin on his joined hands. "*Loups-garous*. You say 'werewolf' to most people in America, they think of Lon Chaney in *The Wolf Man*—weren't they playing that at the Apollo a little while back?"

"I went to see it."

Austin nodded. "It's just *Doctor Jekyll and Mr. Hyde* on a bad hair day." Ariel choked, and he grinned and went on. "Or worse still, people think of those whatchamacallits in the last Bertie Scrubb book, the ponies who turn into boys on the day of the new moon."

"The Pony Pals." Ariel made a face. "I don't read those books."

"Neither do I," said Austin, "but I've got a nine-year-old sister who's crazy about them, so I get to hear all about them whenever I visit." He shuddered, and Ariel laughed again.

"Grandma says it isn't like that at all," he went on, abruptly serious. "Not one bit. People in the old country really are scared of *loups-garous*, or they're supposed to be *loups-garous* themselves. People got tried and burnt at the stake for being werewolves back in the day, the way other people got tried and burnt for witchcraft. I read an old book a few years ago called *The Book of Were-Wolves* by Sabine Baring-Gould, and it talked about how people in rural France into Victorian times still treated werewolves as real."

"And Leonora Blake had something to do in that."

"That's what Grandma says. She said that old Miss Blake—that's what she always calls her—old Miss Blake had some statues and things from old times, and that had something to do with her being a werewolf. She had a bronze plaque with a red moon and wolves on it, I know that much. I heard that the Heydonian's going to have that on display sometime soon."

Ariel gave him a wary look. "Where did you hear that?"

He shrugged. "Mom heard it from somebody she knows who works at the museum. They're not supposed to talk, but—" He shrugged. "That's all I know about it."

"I wonder if you could ask your grandmother about that."

"I can try," said Austin. "Can I have your cell number? That way I can call you if I get something worth your time."

"I don't have a cell phone." Meeting his look of disbelief: "Seriously, I don't. Like I said, I'm old-fashioned. I can give you my land line number. You'll probably have to leave a message but I'll call you back."

"Okay, I can settle for that." He got out his phone, entered the number as she gave it. "Thanks. Do you have email?"

"Yeah, but I check it maybe once a week, at the library."

He laughed. "Okay, you're really old-fashioned. Got it. Do you have a horse tied up outside, to ride home on? Or a coach?"

"I wish," Ariel said, meaning it. "No, I have to settle for a bus." She picked up her coffee cup as a distraction; the coffee was lukewarm, but she drank some anyway.

"Before you catch that bus," said Austin, "any chance I can ask a question or two? You've got me curious." She motioned for him to go on, and he finished his coffee at a gulp and said, "I'd heard plenty about Dr. Moravec but until a couple of months ago nobody ever mentioned that he had any family at all. Then you showed up at the bookstore, and my boss told me that you're his granddaughter. I know it's prying, but I'm curious. So's half of Adocentyn."

"I'm not surprised," Ariel said, amused. "He got married a long time ago, when he lived in Washington DC. It didn't work out, but they had my dad before they broke up. My grandmother took my dad to California with her after the divorce, and then when my dad grew up he came back to this side of the country, got a Ph.D. in accounting, married my mom, and settled down in Summerfield. That's where I'm from. I visited my grandfather here a couple of times when I was little, but my mom doesn't get along with either of Dad's parents so—" She shrugged. "But when I turned eighteen in June I came here to spend the summer with my grandfather, and we got along really well, so I stayed."

"And he hired you."

"I helped him out on a case."

"You're lucky."

"I know." With a sudden smile: "You have no idea how well I know that." She considered him. "You don't live at home."

"Nope. My dad and I disagree about some things. The easiest way to deal with that was for me to move out. I've got a room up above the bookstore—Mrs. Dupois owns the building, and my rent is I do all the maintenance stuff when I'm not on shift—and I go home for dinner every Saturday because Mom's sure I'll starve to death otherwise." He indicated her coffee cup with a gesture. "Ready for that refill?"

"Let me check." She pulled her pocket watch out of her purse, grinned to see him goggle at it in surprise. "Sorry—I need to get going. Can I get the refill sometime later? Maybe once you find out what else your grandmother remembers."

He grinned. "You're good at this. Sure, I'll call you, and you can call me back or drop by the store any time. If it's open, I'm probably there."

Ariel agreed to that, they said their goodbyes, and she left the coffee shop. The thought of catching the next bus straight home appealed, not least because the sky had clouded up and promised rain in the not so distant future, but part of the conversation she'd had with Austin had set her mind racing, and there was one place in downtown Adocentyn she knew she might be able to find out what she needed to know.

A few minutes of zigzagging through downtown streets beneath gray and threatening skies brought her to the vast Egyptian mass of the library. Once inside, she made a beeline to the fourth floor, walked along the card catalog to the section that listed books by subject, and started flipping through the cards in the drawer marked WER-WES. She had to flip past a long sequence of cards marked WEREWOLVES—FICTION, but finally reached WEREWOLVES—FOLKLORE and found the book she wanted:

Baring-Gould, Sabine THE BOOK OF WERE-WOLVES

It took only a few minutes for her to track it down in the stacks. A glance at the table of contents made her nod. She tucked it under her arm, then went back to the subject index and looked up old books on photography.

The sky was darkening as she left the library and started for the transit mall, and all at once she was back in the state of mind she'd practiced with Theophilus Cray. That irritated her for a moment, but she caught herself and turned her full attention to the street around her, the cars and people moving past. If there was somebody following her, she told herself, she needed to know that—and if there was something else she needed to notice, well, that habit worked for Sherlock Holmes, didn't it?

If anyone followed her to the transit mall, there was no sign of it. She boarded the next number 9 bus without incident, rode it to Lyon Avenue, and walked the few blocks home. Questions about werewolves circled in her mind, and so did the hope that the rain would hold off long enough for her to get home unsoaked.

Improbably enough, the first drops hadn't fallen yet when she went up the steps to the familiar door. Her grandfather's house was as silent as she expected; a note on the table let her know that he'd be home very late and she was on her own for dinner. Once she'd changed into comfortable clothes and tucked the paper crow Austin had made for her in the desk drawer next to her shewstone, she went back downstairs, got tea started, closed curtains, turned on a few lights, and settled on the sofa with Sabine Baring-Gould's book.

By the time the teakettle let out its usual yell, she was beginning to wish she'd chosen something else to read. Austin hadn't exaggerated the fear that surrounded werewolves or the stark reality that people in old Europe assigned to them. Baring-Gould's brisk Victorian optimism was seemingly enough to convince him that lycanthropy couldn't be more than a medieval superstition wrapped around the ugly reality of homicidal insanity, but his confidence didn't communicate itself to Ariel. It didn't help that once she got her tea and settled down on the sofa again, the windows rattled suddenly: a gust of wind flinging the first heavy raindrops against the windows, she realized after a minute or so of stark panic, but it took a while for her heart to stop pounding.

She started reading the book again, then closed it with a shudder. Just then, with rain hammering on the windows and an autumn night closing its grip around the little pool of lamplight she inhabited, it was too easy to hear around her in the night the echoes of an older world. All things considered, she realized, it hadn't been that many centuries since people had huddled close around their fires on such nights, dreading things that might be moving through the darkness just beyond the fragile shelter of their homes.

Some of those things had been real. Ariel knew that in her bones, since her encounters with the Unseen had already brought her face to face with more than one ghost, not to mention a witch, a wraith, and a spell meant to kill her.

And werewolves?

She got up suddenly, frowning. Somewhere, not too many months before, she'd read something about werewolves that made sense of the traditional stories in terms of the lore of magic. A book of her grandfather's, or a book from the library? It annoyed her that she couldn't remember, and a glance around the bookshelves didn't offer any clues.

More rain rattled against the windows. She gave the book by Sabine Baring-Gould an uneasy look, sat back down, pulled her e-reader out from under a stack of books on the end table, and found one of her collections of Sherlock Holmes stories. The infallible logic of Arthur Conan Doyle's famous fictional detective helped distract her from the darkness outside, and what might be moving through that darkness. It was a weak distraction, and she knew it, but just for the moment it was enough.

Chapter 10

THE DOG THAT WASN'T THERE

The weather was no better the next morning, and the newspaper announced that the forecast for the next few days was rain, rain, and more rain. Ariel, who had two of those days off from her studies at Aunt Clarice's, stared out the kitchen window at the gray wet sky, grumbled to herself, and called up her friend Jill Callahan in the little town of Criswell, a few miles west of Adocentyn.

As often as her schedule permitted, she liked to take the bus out to Criswell to help at Jill's boarding stable, since the horses that boarded there always needed more exercise than Jill and her stable manager could give them. Forty-four degrees and driving rain wasn't good weather to take horses for a gallop, though. Jill was as understanding about the postponement as Ariel expected, but even so Ariel was in a foul mood when she got off the phone and trudged into the parlor with a cup of coffee.

The book by Sabine Baring-Gould still waited, but even in daylight she found she didn't want to plunge back into the terrifying legends it chronicled. Instead, she started reading one of the library books on 35mm photography, and spent the morning figuring out how to use her new camera. Then, a little after noon, the sky decided to make fools of the weather forecasters, stopped raining, and began to clear off. It was too late for Ariel to bus out to Criswell, but not too late to load a roll of color film into her camera, put on a warm coat and sturdy waterproof shoes, and go outdoors to try her hand at a little nature photography.

The day had turned blustery; scraps of cloud rushed low and fast overhead beneath a pale blue sky, driven by a cold wind. Ariel walked the half block to Culpeper Park, tried to find an easy way over the wet grass to the nearest brick path, then gave up and squelched her way across. Once she was on the path, she glanced back and found that her footprints in the soft ground had already filled up with water. It was a nice image, she thought, and spent a couple of minutes finding interesting angles and snapping four pictures. She had to stop herself from waiting for the image to appear on some nonexistent screen, the way they'd done when she'd taken pictures with her cell phone, and laughed at the difference.

She found three more things to photograph—orange-brown oak leaves on wet grass, a gnarled pine branch with water droplets clinging to the needles, and a crow perched on a leafless branch, looking down irritably at her—before she realized that she wasn't the only person taking pictures that day. A woman in her thirties with ash-blonde highlights in her brown hair, dressed in tight jeans and a nicely tailored brown wool jacket, was going slowly from tree to tree not far away, aiming a much fancier camera up into the branches and taking multiple shots. Ariel glanced at her, wondered why she looked familiar, and then remembered the reason: she'd been at Bill's Cameras the day Ariel had spent dodging Theophilus Cray and someone else.

The argument she'd walked into on that occasion didn't make Ariel especially interested in talking to the woman. She turned away, found another view worth photographing—the skyscrapers of downtown Adocentyn off in the middle distance, still partly swathed by scraps of cloud from the departing storm. Four exposures caught that tolerably well, or so she hoped. She had just lowered the camera from the fourth shot when she realized that the other photographer had come toward her and was standing at a polite distance, waiting.

"Oh, hi," said Ariel.

"Hello," said the woman. She had a stiff, unfriendly look on her face, but she said, "Nice day for photography."

"I hope so," Ariel said. "I'm really new at this."

The woman's face softened a little. "Just starting out?"

Ariel nodded. "Yes. This is my first real camera, and—" She held up the camera, forced a smile. "My first roll of film."

The woman took that in, and allowed a smile. "Well, everyone has to start somewhere. I'm glad to see anybody doing film photography these days."

"You've been doing it for a long time," Ariel ventured.

"Since I was in school." She considered Ariel for a moment. "You were at Bill's Cameras the other day, weren't you?"

"Yes, I was. Did you get the problem with the pictures worked out?"

That got a sudden scowl. "No. I'm still furious about that. It was a perfect shot, the kind of thing you get once in a thousand rolls of film, and right here in Culpeper Park!" She gestured sharply with the hand that wasn't holding her camera. "And every single place I took the negatives told me that the image wasn't on the film. It's enough to make me want to scream, but—" A sudden shrug punctuated the sentence.

"Do you mind telling me what happened?" Ariel asked. When the woman turned an unfriendly glance toward her: "I might have a problem like that one of these days."

"One of these nights," the woman said. She paused, then went on. "I suppose so. I was here in the park about eleven o'clock. I do nature photography, art prints mostly, and the moon was full, so I wanted to get some good black and white night shots. Streetlights on both sides of the park, the moon overhead, lots of deep shadows and the city lights behind it all—it was a good night. I was not too far from here, actually, and I'd just started my third roll when I saw the dog.

"It was—" She gestured over toward a clump of trees nearby. "Just past those trees. A big dog, maybe an Alsatian, just trotting along minding its own business. It was a perfect image. Perfect! So I started shooting. Of course it heard the camera, and it slowed down a little and looked at me with these yellow eyes that reflected the light back at me. Then it trotted away. I used up nearly the entire roll on that dog. And then I took the film to Bill's the next day, and when I picked it up, no dog. It wasn't spoiled film, either. Everything else came through just fine, but the dog wasn't there."

"That's really weird," Ariel said.

"Tell me about it. The rest of the roll came out just fine, so the night wasn't a complete flop, but I wish I'd gotten that dog."

"I bet," said Ariel. "You do this professionally, don't you?"

That got her a look that was almost benevolent. "I wish. Oh, I sell some prints at galleries, but my day job's in real estate. I'm Stacy Kretzler, by the way." She started to put out her hand in greeting.

"I'm Ariel Moravec," said Ariel.

The hand drew back. "Any relation to Dr. Moravec at the Heydonian?"

"He's my grandfather."

The woman didn't quite jump backwards, but the feeling was there. The smile fell off her face and she glared at Ariel. "Then I'm sorry I wasted my time." She turned abruptly and stalked away, leaving Ariel to watch her in bafflement.

A minute or so passed and Stacy Kretzler vanished beyond the trees to the west. Ariel shrugged, wondered what was behind the reaction, and then turned away. A flicker of memory stirred, and she walked over to the nearby clump of trees. Not far past them—she was sure of it—was the muddy area where she'd seen the dog footprints the day she'd gone to speak to Holly Harshaw. She went over to the spot she remembered and found plenty of other tracks through the mud, but a minute or so of searching turned up one of the dog pawprints over to one side, not quite erased. Oddly, for a dog that big, the print went only about half as deep in the mud as the prints of a much smaller dog just a few inches away. Ariel considered it, started to turn away, and then took a picture of the print before going on to other things.

She finished up the roll of film on pictures that pleased her, but her mind kept circling back to the dog that wasn't there and the improbably shallow pawprint. When she was taking a picture of more fallen leaves on wet grass, she remembered that she'd heard another account of a camera that hadn't seen something it should have: the security camera at the Heydonian which hadn't registered someone picking the lock on the door. It didn't seem likely at all that that could have anything in common with the unphotographable dog, but the coincidence unsettled her.

She'd put her camera back in its case, tucked it into her shoulder bag, and started picking her way back from the brick walkway to the sidewalk when another coincidence occurred to her. The evening before, when she was reading Sherlock Holmes instead of *The Book of Were-Wolves*, the great detective had said something about a dog. What was it?

The memory wouldn't surface. Ariel got to the sidewalk and headed for home.

The familiarities of the house on Lyon Avenue surrounded her promptly enough. Once she'd shed coat and outdoor shoes and stowed the camera in its place in her desk, she went downstairs, got tea started, and opened the volume of Sherlock Holmes stories she'd been reading the evening before. It took her a few minutes to find the passage about the dog, but once she did she read it twice. Inspector Gregory, one of the less clueless of Holmes's official foils, was questioning the detective:

> "Is there any other point to which you would wish to draw my attention?"
> "To the curious incident of the dog in the night-time."

> "The dog did nothing in the night-time."
>
> "That was the curious incident," remarked Sherlock Holmes.

Well, I've got another curious incident, Ariel thought. This dog didn't do anything, either, including showing up on film. What does that imply?

The teakettle interrupted her then. She brooded over the mysterious dog while she was making tea, and by the time she came back to the parlor with a cup in her hand she had the first whisper of an idea about what it might mean. Since there was nothing she could do with that knowledge just then and no way to find out more until her grandfather came home that evening, she set the idea aside for the moment and spent the next few hours translating her shorthand scrawls from Aunt Clarice's talks on herbs into something she was sure she'd be able to interpret a few months down the line.

She had finished that task and was trying to nerve herself up to plunge back into Sabine Baring-Gould's book on werewolves when the front door rattled and Dr. Moravec came in. While he was shedding his coat, she got up, got the teakettle started again, and then flopped back onto the couch to wait for him. Once he'd nodded a greeting, settled on his chair with his legs stretched out, closed his eyes for a little while and opened them again, she said, "I may have talked to somebody else who's seen Gerard Breyer's mystery dog."

Dr. Moravec considered her with one eyebrow raised. "Go on."

"The problem is it's a person named Stacy Kretzler, and I don't think she likes you."

"A considerable understatement," said Dr. Moravec. "How on earth did you happen to meet her?"

"She saw me taking pictures in Culpeper Park and came over to talk. We ran into each other once before then, too." She sketched out the conversation she'd overheard at the camera store. The moment she mentioned the unphotographable dog, Dr. Moravec folded his hands and allowed a very slight smile.

The teakettle chose that moment to interrupt again, and she got up, fixed tea for both of them, and came back out into the parlor. Her grandfather thanked her gravely for the cup, waited until she was seated again, and said, "But do go on."

Ariel gave him an uncertain look, but finished describing her first encounter with Stacy Kretzler, and then went on to recount what had happened in Culpeper Park that afternoon. When she wound up her account with Kretzler's sudden departure, he allowed a chuckle.

"Yes, I imagine she would. Stacy Kretzler's descended through her mother from one of the old Adocentyn families. Six years ago she came to the Heydonian with a small collection of old books on magic she wanted to sell to us. They had been in her family for a while, she said. The trustees asked me to investigate, and it turned out that all of them had been stolen from the Heydonian by one of Kretzler's grandparents, back when the library didn't have the kind of security system it does now. Since the statute of limitations was long past, of course, there was no question of criminal charges, but our lawyers negotiated with hers, we recovered the books, and Kretzler got a modest finder's fee instead of the very large payment she'd convinced herself she deserved." He sipped tea.

"How did she take that?"

"Not well. At the time, certainly, she insisted to anyone that would listen that I had personally cheated her out of half a million dollars. The books weren't worth anything close to that, but I'm sure you can imagine how she behaved to people who tried to tell her that."

Ariel nodded. "That makes sense. Do you think the dog she saw was the same one that Gerard Breyer's been seeing?"

"I think it's quite possible," said Dr. Moravec.

Ariel waited for him to go on. When he didn't, she gave him an uncharitable look and reached for her teacup.

"I noticed," he said then, "that you've been reading Sabine Baring-Gould's interesting little study on werewolves. Would it be fair to ask why?"

"Sure," said Ariel. "I bought some of Leonora Blake's books at Dupois and Company a few days ago, and I got into a conversation with one of the clerks who works there. He said his grandmother used to know her. We got together for coffee on Monday, and he said—" She stopped, then made herself go on despite the ridiculousness of the words: "He said that his grandmother told him that Leonora Blake was a werewolf."

The old man's eyebrows went up, but all he said was, "That's very interesting."

Ariel considered him for a moment. "Was she?"

"Not to my knowledge, no."

Another moment passed. "Okay," said Ariel. "This business about Gerard Breyer's dog and the rest of it," she went on. "Are we talking about—" She had to push past her own reluctance to say the word again. "Werewolves?"

"Good. That's one of the things I still have to determine." He held up a hand, forestalling her next words. "And until certain other things happen, or don't happen, I'd rather not discuss the matter further. There are several other things the dog could be, and it's much more likely that it's one of those. Once we know for certain, we can take the necessary steps—and if it does turn out we're dealing with a werewolf, then the two of us will have to make some preparations. There may be significant dangers involved, you know."

"That's what Baring-Gould said," said Ariel.

"There are better sources," said her grandfather. "In fact, you read one not that many months ago. Still—" His hand forestalled her again. "We can discuss that later." He reached inside his jacket, pulled out a folded document. "In the meantime, you may find this interesting."

She took it and unfolded it. It turned out to be a magazine article about the Kynokefale machine; somebody had cut it from the magazine and stapled it in one corner. She thanked him and tried not to look too irritable.

Aside from dinner, which they ate together as usual, he spent most of the evening in his study, brooding over volumes of magical lore. Ariel decided she wasn't ready for any more of Baring-Gould's werewolf lore yet, and plunged into the article on the Kynokefale machine. It was a pleasant little puff piece with big color photos, one of the corroded mass that was all that was left of the machine when archeologists dug it out of the wreckage of an ancient Greek city, one of the reconstruction that scholars at a midwestern university had built, a suitcase-sized rectangle of wood and gleaming metal, open on both ends to show glimpses of the gears and shafts inside. The text chattered about how only two such machines had been found so far, one in the ocean off the island of Antikythera, the other in ruins near the town of Kynokefale, and speculated about whether more might still exist in Greece or elsewhere.

The article didn't take her long to finish. Afterward she plunged into Leonora Blake's first novel, *Pilgrimage to Montségur*—another lively romantic adventure set in the south of France, nearly as good as *The Chapel of the Grail*. By the end of the first chapter she'd decided to make finding a copy of Blake's third novel a priority. She got through the first half of it before the grandfather clock reminded her that she had plans for the morning.

By the time she went upstairs and sat at her desk for her second practice of the day, werewolves were far from her thoughts. Toward the end of the scrying session, though, she saw the image of a wolf again, running among trees that looked uncomfortably like the ones in Culpeper Park. That left her with tangled feelings: pleased that she'd gotten another clear image in the shewstone, unnerved because of the subject. It took her longer than usual to get to sleep, and during the night she dreamed more than once of hiding from wolves.

Chapter 11

AN ACT OF MAGIC

The next morning dawned clear and cool, with a sharp autumn chill in the air. Ariel woke early to find the first splash of sunlight on her bedroom wall. As soon as she thought Jill Callahan would be awake, she called and made sure it would be a good day to come help with the horses. Nine o'clock duly found her lodged in a seat on the number 38 bus as it lumbered patiently through Adocentyn's western neighborhoods. Half a dozen suburbs and as many little farm towns later, the bus rolled to a stop in Criswell, and Ariel shouldered a duffel bag and set out on foot the rest of the way to a familiar farmhouse.

When she boarded the same bus for the ride back to Adocentyn a little more than six hours later, her muscles yelled at her every time she moved them. She wondered how long it would take before she could ride all day without hobbling afterwards, the way Jill and her stable manager Ricky Higgins did, then reminded herself that they rode every day and she didn't. That dispiriting reflection made her flee for distraction to the book she'd brought with her, the volume of Leonora Blake's poetry she'd picked up at Dupois & Company. She read a few of the poems, and liked them, but her thoughts strayed in other directions: mostly, to her surprise, to Austin Wronski and the guarded but pleasant conversation they'd had.

She was still thinking about him when the bus reached Elmhurst, a suburb old enough that it had its own little business district with a half dozen shops, a post office, and a few other nondescript buildings. The bus lurched to a stop there to let off two of the handful of other people on board, and take on someone else. Ariel glanced up and realized to her surprise that she knew the newcomer: Holly Harshaw's son. He had a jacket and a tie on, both looking like they'd seen a lot of wear, and a battered briefcase in one hand; the bright sunlight made the mottled coloring of his skin even more obvious than before. He spotted her once he'd paid his fare and came tentatively toward her. She sent a smile his way, hoping that it would encourage him to sit near her. He promptly sat in the seat in front of her and turned to face her.

"Kyle, right?" Ariel said.

"Yeah. Any luck with the plaque?"

She nodded. "We managed to sort out the provenance and the provenience." His blank look told her that he didn't know the words, so she amended: "Who owned it and where they got it from. I haven't heard if the Heydonian's made an offer on it yet but I'm pretty sure they will."

"I bet," he said. A silence passed as the bus lumbered around a corner. "I want to see it once it's on display. Mom used to tell me some really odd stories about that when I was a kid."

"What kind of stories?"

"Stuff about werewolves." With a sidelong look: "I'm sure you don't believe in those."

Ariel shrugged, imitating a lack of interest she didn't feel. "I get the sense the world doesn't care what I believe or not."

That got her another sidelong glance. "I won't argue with that." Then, after a pause: "Mom said that it used to belong to people who were werewolves. It was something sacred to them. She said her dad told her that. I never had the chance to ask him about it myself because he wouldn't talk to me at all." He considered her. "Any chance you took a look at his will?"

"Yeah," Ariel admitted. "That was part of the research I did."

"So you know he left Mom the house but otherwise cut her off." She nodded. He spent a long moment with his mouth tensed, as though trying to decide how much to tell her, then said, "I'm the reason. Mom was a party girl when she was young, did a lot of wild stuff, and finally she got knocked up and didn't have any idea who the dad was. The family wanted her to get an abortion but she wouldn't do it—she said she could tell I was a person already. So she had me, and—" He gestured at himself. "I didn't have the vitiligo when I was born, but everybody took one look at me and they knew my dad wasn't white. Uncle Clarence was a major jerk about it, but Grandpa Jasper was way past that. He didn't just have a cow, he had a whole herd."

"Ouch," said Ariel. "I hope you and your mom don't have too much trouble."

"Oh, we get by okay." A hard-edged smile twisted his face. "Doing a lot better these days than Uncle Clarence." Ariel had to fight to keep her reaction off her face, but he'd glanced away by then. "Grandma Lizzie had some money of her own and left it to Mom, along with her shares in the Heydonian—yeah, Mom's a shareholder, to the extent of eight whole shares. And after she had me, Mom got serious about things, dropped out of the party scene, took classes in bookkeeping, and got a business going. It pays the bills, and I work for her these days." He patted the briefcase. "That's what I'm doing now: picking up paperwork from one of her clients. I do a lot of data entry, too. It's a job, and the free rent helps."

"I live with my grandfather," Ariel admitted.

"Lots of people I went to school with are living at home." He shrugged, fell silent.

A block or so of suburb slid past. "Do you know anything else about the werewolves and the plaque?" Ariel asked finally.

"Not a lot. The plaque's from somewhere in Italy, and that's where the werewolves are supposed to be from. I think Mom knows more than she wants to talk about. There's a lot she won't say about when she was younger."

Ariel considered that. After another pause: "But the plaque means a lot to her."

"Yeah. She talks about that sometimes."

The bus pulled up to a stop at a park and ride lot, and more than a dozen people boarded. Some of them sat down close to Ariel and Kyle, and he got a rueful look on his face, sent an apologetic glance Ariel's way, and turned to face forward. Other than a distracted goodbye when they both left the bus at the downtown Adocentyn transit mall, that was the end of the conversation. He headed for the stop for the number 11 bus, which ran north of Culpeper Park, while she went to her usual stop and caught a number 9 bus a few minutes later.

When she left the bus on Lyon Street and started on the three uphill blocks to home, Ariel was pleased to find that her muscles were less irate than she'd expected. On the way out to Criswell that morning, she'd thought of one way to try to get a copy of Leonora Blake's third novel; that felt important, though she couldn't tell why. She paused at her grandfather's house just long enough to drop off the duffel, then walked the few blocks to the Culpeper Hill branch of the Adocentyn Public Library and made a beeline for the desk with computers that gave access to a statewide library catalogue.

A quarter hour of searching left her feeling annoyed. Two libraries in the state had copies of *The Chapel of the Grail* that could be checked out, and one in Summerfield had a copy of *Pilgrimage to Montségur* that was library use only, but nobody had a copy of *The Carnelian Moon*. Fuming, she tried the places she knew online where you could sometimes get electronic copies of old books, and drew a blank at each of them. Finally she gave up and went home.

The telephone had better news for her when she checked messages: Austin Wronski had called to say he'd made time to talk with his grandmother about Leonora Blake. She called him back at once, and was startled and pleased that he picked up. "Yeah, I'm off work at four most days," he said. "Any chance you're free sometime soon?" She checked her schedule, they settled on the next day at four at the same coffee shop, and chatted a little before hanging up.

Brief as it was, the conversation left her feeling unexpectedly cheerful. The change in mood stayed with her through the evening. Her grandfather's silence—he was deep in thought all that evening, and said fewer than a dozen words to her from the time he came home to the time she went up the stairs for the night—didn't dent it, nor did a couple of chapters of Baring-Gould's book on werewolves, which she made time to read before dinner. She decided that a pleasant day spent riding was responsible, and thought no more of it.

After dinner, it was dark and cold enough that more werewolf lore didn't appeal, so she settled down on the sofa to finish *Pilgrimage to Montségur*. Afterward she brooded a little over Leonora Blake's third novel, and a stray memory reminded her of something she'd read in one of the old books on scrying her grandfather had given her. Later still, once she'd gone up to her room, she pulled the book off its place on her bookshelf, perched on her bed and read the passage she remembered. If you wanted to find something and there didn't seem to be any earthly way to get it, you could imagine it intently in the crystal, build up an image in the astral light, and cause it to be drawn to you like iron filings to a magnet: that was what the book said.

Ariel read the instructions through twice, and decided that she was willing to try it, even though it was from a chapter full of practices she hadn't gotten to yet. Her grandfather had talked about some of the problems with skipping ahead in the book but hadn't actually forbidden her to do that, she reminded herself, and tried not to notice the prevarication.

She did her ordinary practice first with no more results than usual. Then, after writing up the details and reading the instructions one more time, she stared into the crystal again and tried to imagine a copy of *The Carnelian Moon*. It would be a hardback, she decided, about the same size as *The Chapel of the Grail*, with the same kind of cloth on the covers and the same font for the title and the author. She could almost see it, the paper yellowed with age, the covers scuffed a little at the edges—

Then, just for an instant, the "almost" went away and she could see it in the crystal, just as clearly as though she was looking at a photograph. The cloth on the cover was green instead of the blue of *The Chapel of the Grail*, the font of the title a little different, and there was a light brown stain low down on the front cover. An eyeblink later it was gone, and further attempts didn't bring it back. Ariel put five minutes into the effort anyway, then wrote up what she'd experienced, put the shewstone and her practice journal away, and got ready for bed wondering whether she'd accomplished anything or not.

The next morning she left for Aunt Clarice's shop beneath a rumpled gray sky. A hard freeze overnight had left white frost on the lawns and shrubs she passed, and enough of the chill remained to turn her breath into puffs of white mist as she walked. The air inside the shop, freighted with the scents of hot wax and herbal oils, seemed almost stifling by comparison, though the warmth was welcome.

That day was a busy one, with candles to dress with oil and set burning, spell papers to write and fold just so, and an herbal product to sort and package. The big brown bag of five-finger grass—cinquefoil, Ariel reminded herself, that was what her grandfather's books called it—had to be emptied a little at a time, and the tangled mass of herbs put into a big steel bowl. Then a small amount of the herb had to go into each of an endless stack of little plastic bags with labels on them. It was familiar work after two months of practice, and the herb itself had a pleasant dry-hay smell that reminded Ariel of horse barns.

Later on, Aunt Clarice sat the two of them down in the little alcove in the back of the shop and talked about the magical uses of cinquefoil. There were plenty of those, enough to keep her talking for more than an hour. "Five-finger grass," she said, "can stop any evil that five fingers can get up to." She illustrated the point with half a dozen stories of curses and evil spells she'd broken with this or that preparation of the herb. Ariel copied it all down in shorthand that was starting to flow a little more easily. The whole time, though, she had to struggle to keep her attention on the herb. Her thoughts kept trying to wander off toward the old clock on the wall, the end of the day's lessons, and her appointment with Austin Wronski.

It was a little more than half past three when Aunt Clarice shooed them out of the shop, and Ariel chatted a little with Cassie about the movie the next evening, said her goodbyes, and set off for the transit mall. The lessons she'd learned from Theophilus Cray came to mind promptly, and so did the lesson of the fern spores. What am I not noticing? Ariel asked herself, and made an effort to pay more attention than usual to the places she passed and the people who shared the sidewalk with her.

She got to the coffee shop a little before four o'clock. Austin hadn't arrived yet, so she got an Americano with cream and sugar and chose a place to sit with a good view of the door. As she took a second sip of the coffee she spotted him through the window, and a moment later he was through the door. He went to the counter, ordered a cup of something, and then crossed to where she was sitting while the barista made it up. "I was supposed to get you that one."

She met his smile with one of her own. "You can get the second one. I've got more time this afternoon."

He nodded, went back to the counter to get his coffee, and then returned and settled in the seat facing her. "Good. I promise I won't spend so much time veering off on tangents."

Ariel considered that and said, "Okay. But I may not hold you to that."

Nor did she. It was just past six o'clock when she finally crossed the street to the transit mall and caught the next route 9 bus out Ivy Street. During that time he'd told her what he'd learned from his grandmother—nothing Ariel hadn't learned already, except for a few details about Leonora Blake's travels in Italy and Spain—but they'd also talked about any number of other things, from gossip about the Heydonian to droll stories about customers at Dupois & Company to some of his difficulties with his family and some her difficulties with hers.

Twice in the course of the conversation he'd asked something about her grandfather, and both times she'd smiled and held up a warning finger, and he'd blushed and apologized, which was charming in its way. All through the conversation, he'd smiled at her often, and he'd complimented her more than once, in an offhand manner she found just as charming. It had been, all told, two very pleasant hours, and they'd finished it up by agreeing to meet again for coffee a few days later.

Once aboard the bus, Ariel settled back into the seat and let herself bask for a little while in thoughts about the conversation. Around the time the bus rolled past the old town green with its statue of Elias Ashmole, she blinked and shook herself as though she'd just woken up. It had been two years since she'd last gotten a crush on a boy, but she recognized the feeling.

Well, why not? That was the first thought that surfaced as she considered Austin and her feelings. He's smart, he's nice, he's as much of a book geek as I am, and he doesn't talk down to me or get uncomfortable because I'm not like everyone else: those were the thoughts that followed it. Whatever else happened or didn't happen, she could certainly meet him again for coffee and conversation, and if things worked out, maybe something a little fancier, like an old movie at the Apollo ...

She realized just in time that the bus was closing in on her stop, and pulled the bell. A minute or so later she was on the sidewalk, and once the bus rattled onward she hurried through the gathering dusk up Lyon Avenue to the comfortable silence of the big green house. Her grandfather wasn't home yet when she got there, though she'd been inside for maybe ten minutes at most and was just fixing her first cup of tea when the front door rattled and he came in.

She glanced through the doorway from the kitchen once he'd shed coat and hat and settled in his usual chair, then fixed a second cup of tea for him and brought both cups out. That earned her a nod of thanks, and she grinned and settled on her side of the sofa, guessing that he'd say something when he was ready.

She was right, too, though it was most of five minutes before he broke his silence. "Well," he said. "The Harshaw estate is being difficult about the Faliscan plaque."

"I hope they'll let it be part of the exhibit," said Ariel.

"Fortunately, yes. They've agreed to loan it to us for the duration, but they're asking for quite a bit more money than the plaque is really worth. We made a counteroffer that they rejected. I don't expect their next offer to be much more reasonable than the first."

Ariel nodded.

"Everything else is as it should be, fortunately. The rest of the items haven't given us any significant trouble, and preparations for the exhibition are ahead of schedule. It's all very busy there just now, with workmen going in and out. But there's another detail I need to pass on." He reached into a pocket, brought out a small brown paper bag that contained something flat. "Theophilus gave me something for you." He handed over the bag. Ariel reached across the coffee table to take it. "He told me he had a sense that you were looking for a copy of this, and wanted to offer it as a gift."

Inside was a hardback book in an old-fashioned green cloth binding. Ariel pulled it out of the bag and stared at it in amazement. It was a copy of Leonora Blake's third novel,

The Carnelian Moon. It looked identical, down to the fine details, to the one she'd seen in her shewstone the night before. Even the light brown stain on the cover was there.

Astonished, she looked from the book to her grandfather and back again. His expression was no more decipherable than usual, and she wondered in a sudden burst of embarrassment if he knew that she'd tried to cast a spell to get a copy. Abruptly she realized that she needed to say something. "I—I'll thank him. Should I send a card?"

A quick shake of his head denied it. "Just mention it when you next see him."

"I'll do that," she said.

Dr. Moravec nodded. "Excellent. One other question needs to be settled soon, by the way. As a trustee of the Heydonian I need to attend the opening reception for the new exhibition." He named the date, just over a week away. "One of the benefits I get in exchange is that I'm allotted a certain number of guest passes. It's a semiformal event, suits and ties for men, cocktail dresses for women, but I seem to recall you have something along those lines. Are you interested?"

"Sure," said Ariel. Then, to her own surprise, she found herself asking, "Would it be okay for me to get a second guest pass for a friend?"

Dr. Moravec nodded. "Of course. I'll let the office know."

CHAPTER *12*

THE WOLVES IN THE FOREST

Later that evening, after dinner, Ariel took the copy of *The Carnelian Moon* up to her room and sat on one side of her bed for a while, staring at the book's cover, seeing all the details exactly where they'd been in the image in the crystal the night before. Come on, she told herself. You already knew that magic works.

By the time she'd finished the thought, though, she knew that it wasn't the reality of magic that troubled her. No, the question that circled down somewhere deep in her thoughts was whether she'd had any right to use magic to get the book. All things considered, she wondered, was getting Cray to give it to her by magic all that different from stealing it from his library? She thought of the witch Olive Kellinger, and then of Clarence Harshaw: they'd both used magic to get what they wanted, at other people's expense. The fact that both of them had ended up dead as a result did nothing to make the subject any less uncomfortable to her.

The thought of going to her grandfather, confessing her mistake, and asking for his advice occurred to her, but the thought made her cringe with shame. She spent a short time wondering if she should give the book back to Theophilus Cray, and then a briefer time still wondering if she should back away from magical training before she did something unforgivable.

No, she decided finally. No, neither of those are the right thing to do—but I need to think a lot harder before I try anything like that again.

The book went into her bookshelf next to Leonora Blake's other novels. She turned, sat at her desk, got out her shewstone and practice journal, and set things up for her evening practice. Before she made the opening gesture she considered the crystal, thought about apologizing for what she'd done, and then wrestled for a moment with the uncomfortable thought that nobody might be listening. She sighed, shook her head, and started her practice.

The next day she and Cassie spent the morning turning half a dozen herbs and a box of red cloth bags into protective tobies, packaging them in little plastic bags, and stapling gaudy cardboard tops to them. During the afternoon, Aunt Clarice taught them the basics of dealing with clients: which questions to ask and which to avoid, how to get a silent client to talk and how to get a chatterbox to get to the point, and how to tell when a client was lying outright. That held even more of Ariel's interest than usual. The squiggles of shorthand still felt awkward and sprawled unevenly from her pen, but a glance back up each page of the steno pad when she finished writing reassured her that she would be able to read the notes later on.

On the walk home she and Cassie talked about the movie and settled their plans for the evening. As she half expected, a note lay on the kitchen table, letting her know that her grandfather was at the Heydonian until late and she was on her own for dinner. On the big clock in the parlor, the dial that tracked lunar phases showed the moon only one day from its full. That sent a brief pointless chill down her back, as images from *The Wolf Man* and *The Book of Were-Wolves* came to mind. She pushed them aside, went upstairs, pulled *The Carnelian Moon* from her bookshelf, took it downstairs and started reading.

It turned out to be another atmospheric between-the-wars tale of ancient magic. The main character was another American woman fleeing from an unhappy love affair. The setting was a little mountain village near the border between France and Italy. Ruins of a temple on a hill nearby and curious inscriptions in the village church fed the haunting quality of the tale, but she was three chapters into the story before the main character glimpsed a doglike shadow skulking through the night and gave Ariel her first hint about the story's real theme. She put the book down then and made dinner. Afterwards, with another hour to go before it was time to leave for the theater, she gave the novel a sidelong look, then sighed and picked it up again. Werewolves were the last thing she wanted to think about just then, but the story was too good to set aside.

She had time to read two more chapters before the clock warned her that it was time to go, and by then she was sure that the story was about werewolves. She bundled herself into a warm coat and left the house at a brisk pace. The sun had set well before then and the clouds of the morning had long since blown elsewhere, leaving stars splashed across the blackness above. A cold wind came up from the harbor to hiss among the bare branches of Culpeper Park as she headed down Lyon Avenue. The moon was rising above distant roofs to the east, throwing long pale shadows wherever the streetlights didn't blot them out.

They'd arranged to meet out in front of the Apollo Theater, but as Ariel came down the slope she saw two familiar figures at the corner of Lyon and March, one short and stocky, the other tall and thin. Cassie waved to her when Ariel got within range, but Orion had his phone pressed to his ear and was staring at nothing in particular.

"Yeah," he said finally. "Yeah, I'm good." After a pause. "Yeah, I'll be early. Wednesday at seven, right? See you there." He tapped the screen, grinned, and let out a whoop.

"Okay," said Ariel. "What is it?"

"I'm in a band."

"Seriously? That's the bee's knees. What kind of band?"

"Come on," Cassie said, with a motion of her head. "You can talk on the way. I don't want to miss the start of the movie."

"It's a garage band," Orion admitted as they began walking down the hill. "They just changed the name to Smudge and the Memelords." Ariel choked, remembering the white cat who'd launched a thousand memes, and Orion grinned at her again. "It's an improvement," he said. "The keyboard guy they used to have always wanted to play metal, so they called themselves Rektum, with a K."

Ariel choked again. "What kind of music will you be playing?"

"It's going to be a Seventies tribute band." Ariel gave him a sidelong look and he shrugged. "It's a start, right? I can do something more my style once I've got a reputation. Besides, Billy Joel and Elton John did some great piano licks."

"Well, congratulations," said Ariel. "And keep me posted."

"I'll do that," said Orion. "Fair warning, though—we'll mostly be playing south of Coopers Bay. It's a Southie band."

"Most of the good bands are," said Cassie.

"Well, but—" Orion said, and stopped.

Ariel thought she could guess what the issue was, and a piece of Jazz Age slang she'd never before had the chance to use came to mind. "Orion, don't be a sap. I hang out with you and Cassie, don't I?"

Cassie and Orion looked at each other. "Yeah," said Orion, "but South can take some getting used to."

"Then I'll get used to it," said Ariel. Cassie and Orion looked at each other again.

By then they were too close to the ticket window to keep the conversation going. They got their tickets, bought popcorn at the counter in the lobby, and found a line of three decent seats toward the back of the theater. After a few minutes, the lights went down, the curtains slid open, and Audrey Hepburn climbed out of a taxi in a little black dress. Thereafter, until the lights came on again, Ariel had nothing to worry about besides the absurd misadventures of Audrey Hepburn's character Holly Golightly and the other odd characters of the film.

Once the three of them left the theater to walk home, though, Ariel said, "I hope the business with Andy Rooney wasn't a problem."

"Him playing a Japanese guy? Nah." Cassie shook her head and chuckled. "One of my mom's uncles came to the US back in the Sixties and did a lot of bit parts in Hollywood. You wouldn't believe how many times he played somebody Native American in cowboy movies. You took whatever parts paid your bills."

"Besides," said Orion, "if he wants to make fun of the Japanese, I won't complain."

Ariel sent an uncertain look his way.

"They owned Korea until after the Second World War," said Cassie, "and they were pretty brutal about it. There are stories in Mom's family." She shrugged. "One of those things."

A block or so passed before any of them spoke again, but when the silence broke they started chatting on other subjects. Once they got past the little district of restaurants and bars near the theater, the night turned quiet and the traffic started to thin.

A few more blocks brought them to the intersection where they'd met on the way down. "Well, that was fun," Cassie said. "See you Monday, bright and early."

"Early," said Ariel. "We'll see about bright."

Cassie laughed, and she and Orion turned down March Street. Ariel kept going uphill on Lyon Avenue. The moon was well up in the eastern sky, and shone down cold and bright. She glanced up at it and hurried the rest of the way home.

Once the night was shut safely outside and she'd changed into baggy sweats, she made a cup of tea and settled on the sofa. Despite her words on the way down the hill, the gap between her childhood in Summerfield and the Jacksons' in South Adocentyn felt as wide as the Grand Canyon. She decided she didn't want to face that just then, and picked up *The Carnelian Moon*.

At the end of the next chapter, she stopped and gave the book a long uneasy look. It wasn't that the story had to do with werewolves, though that cut too close to another set of worries for her comfort. It was that the heart of the plot, the carnelian moon of the title, was an object the Heydonian was about to put in its museum. A bronze plaque from the Faliscan country of ancient Italy, with two wolves flanking a disk of red carnelian and three words below it in an antique alphabet, one of them the word for "wolves," the other two unknown: it was the same plaque, the one Leonora Blake had owned.

Ariel read on. Around the plaque, a treasure once guarded by an ancient werewolf cult, an intricate and haunting story of love, fear, and adventure wound its way to a conclusion so unexpected Ariel had no clear sense of how the story would end until she reached the last five pages. Then, on the page that followed the end of the story, a final surprise: black and white photos of the front and back of the Faliscan plaque she knew. No question, it was the same one, with the same three obscure words on the front, copied in ordinary letters below the image, and the same paper label with C117 on it on the upper right corner of the back. The Roman shorthand scratched on the back was considerably clearer than she remembered it, though, and that, too, had been copied under the image: *C. Annaeus Crantor, Sorano donum versipellibus.*

She turned the page, wondering if there would be any further surprises. All she found, on the back of the page with the images, were two sentences in very small print: *Collection of Jacques Hirschberg, Lyon, 1938. Photographs used by permission.* Ariel considered that, then turned back to the images of the plaque and tried to remember what her grandfather and Dr. O'Shaughnessy had said about the inscription on the back. Something wasn't right about the image, she was sure of it, but she was tired enough that the problem wouldn't come clear.

She was still brooding over the image when the rattle of the front door announced Dr. Moravec's return. She knew his ways well enough not to speak to him until he'd shed his coat, gotten the teakettle going, and settled on his chair, but it took an effort to rein herself in and then say no more than, "Can we talk?"

"Of course." Considering her: "I gather it's of some importance."

"It might be," said Ariel. She handed him the book, open to the photographs of the plaque, and watched as he read it and his eyebrows rose.

"*Versipellibus*," he said then. "I wonder. Do you know what it means?" She shook her head, and he went on. "From the werewolves. *Versipellis* is someone who changes his skin, and that was what werewolves were called in classical Latin."

"So we really are dealing with werewolves," said Ariel.

"Excellent. Yes, we are, and I'm fairly sure at this point I know what's behind this whole business. I wonder if you've gotten that far."

"I don't know," she said. "But I think—" Maybe it was the novel she'd just finished, but one possibility leaped to mind at once. "I think one of them is after the plaque."

He nodded. "That's my working hypothesis at this point. If that's the case, I expect an attempt to steal it to be made tomorrow night, when the moon is full."

"Okay," said Ariel. "But—" She stopped, unsure of herself.

Dr. Moravec waited, his face inscrutable.

"I don't think a person can really turn into a wolf."

"You ought to remember what Eliphas Lévi had to say about that," he replied.

She glanced up at him, tried to remember what the old French wizard had put into his book on magic, one of the first volumes she'd read under her grandfather's guidance. "There was a lot in there," she said.

Dr. Moravec nodded. "You'll want to reread it sometime soon. You recall, I hope, that each of us has a body made of the astral light along with the ordinary body of flesh and blood."

She nodded, and he went on. "Under some circumstances it's possible to detach part of the astral body and then shift your mind and awareness into the detached part, using it as a body by itself. People who have out-of-body experiences do that, usually without knowing how they've done it or even what they've done. A competent mage can do the same thing deliberately, and use the separated astral body to travel in this world or others."

"You can do that," she ventured.

"Of course. I don't do it often, but when there's need, yes."

She nodded again, said, "Okay."

"But there's always more than one way to do a thing in magic. The art of astral projection, creating an astral duplicate of your own body, isn't the only option. There's another practice, a very ancient one, that creates a body that isn't human.

"Think back thousands of years ago." His hands splayed out, gesturing, scattering the modern world to the winds. "Most people lived in little villages surrounded by wilderness. They lived much closer to nature than most of us can even imagine today. They knew the habits and the ways of the animals of the wilderness as well as they knew the habits of their human neighbors, and so some of them, those who knew the magical traditions that existed in those days, learned to shape their astral bodies into animal forms.

"They didn't just use their own astral substance, because they wanted a body that could affect ordinary matter. So they drew astral substance from the forest and power from the moon, used amulets taken from the body of the animal, and created animal bodies for themselves. The choice of animal varied from region to region, of course, and there were always different traditions even in the same place, but in ancient Europe five or six thousand years ago, one of the most common forms was the wolf."

"So werewolves," said Ariel.

"Exactly. In those days the bravest of the young men left their villages for a time to go deep into the forest and study with wolf-shamans, old men who dressed in wolfskins and wore necklaces of wolf claws and teeth. The training was so harsh that some of the young men died, but the ones who survived became fierce warriors and skilled hunters, masters of woodcraft and the ways of the forest, honored members of their communities. When the moon was full they would strip naked, rub certain ointments on their bodies, put on wolfskin belts with buckles that had nine tongues, and go into deep trance. That allowed them to project themselves in wolf-form, and go running through the forest to hunt.

"They could kill prey in wolf-form, you see, though they could also make themselves insubstantial enough to pass through walls. They would come back from hunts in their wolf-forms, and wake the next morning with blood on their lips and mud on their hands and feet. Of course there were also risks; ordinary weapons couldn't harm them, but silver, the magical metal of the moon, was another matter. Strike the wolf-form with a silver weapon and the human body back in the village would be found dead in the morning.

"So that was the old wolf-magic, or as much of it as anyone knows now. For century after century they were honored and feared. Then—" He shrugged. "Times changed, the forests were cut down, more villages sprang up. Hunting gave way to herding and farming. The wolf-shamans became outcasts, feared but no longer honored. New religions arrived, and their followers insisted that the old wolf-magic belonged to the devil, along with every other kind of magic the priests didn't control. It's a familiar story."

He fell silent. Ariel waited for a little while and then asked, "Are people who can do that kind of thing still around?"

"Astral shapeshifters? In some parts of the world, yes. There are practitioners of leopard magic in Africa, coyote magic in some parts of Latin America, bear magic in Siberia—

it wouldn't surprise me if Theophilus knows a good deal more about that latter than I do. But the ancient European wolf-cults themselves? If they still exist, nobody seems to know about it. The last of them might have been wiped out in the days of the witch burnings, or in Europe's endless bitter wars. Or there might be a few scattered here and there, still in hiding, the way they must have been during the days of the Inquisition. I wish I knew."

He shook his head and fell silent. Ariel considered him for a while and said, "So what are you going to do?"

"I've already made certain arrangements," Dr. Moravec said. "I know the vulnerabilities of that kind of astral form, and I've researched the traditions of lycanthropy in quite some detail over the last few weeks. There will be certain dangers involved, but nothing I haven't faced many times before."

"And if I want to help?"

Dark eyes regarded her. "I'm far from sure you're prepared for that."

Ariel considered that, and waited for him to say more. Instead, he got up and started for the kitchen, then stopped and turned toward her. "On a more pleasant subject, I believe you wanted these." He extracted an envelope from inside his jacket, and handed it to her.

Ariel opened it and found two guest passes for the opening night reception of the *Artifacts of Ancient Magic* exhibition at the Heydonian Museum. That cheered her, especially when she thought of who she meant to take to the reception. She thanked Dr. Moravec, and he nodded and went into the kitchen to fix tea.

Outside the parlor window, the night deepened. As she settled back on the sofa, Ariel thought about things that were not quite wolves running through the darkness, and shivered.

Later still, when she went up to her room, she gave Nicodemus a long uncertain look. The stuffed wolf sat placidly enough at the foot of her bed, pink tongue lolling between white felt teeth. Harmless? She recalled the gory tales in Baring-Gould's book, and shuddered. Maybe, she thought, the people of the villages had good reason to treat the wolf-shamans as outcasts. That made her shiver again. Shoving aside the thought, she sat down at her desk and forced her attention to the shewstone and her evening practice.

Chapter 13

A BLADE OF SILVER

The next morning Ariel woke up out of dark tangled dreams to a set of perplexities no less tangled. What she could see of the sky through her bedroom windows was gray and rumpled, as though someone had forgotten to iron the clouds. She stayed under the covers for a little while, then made herself get up and stumble through the first part of her morning routine. Her morning practice was a waste of time, as far as she could tell, but she gritted her teeth and made herself sit through five minutes of staring at an empty shewstone. She recognized the problem, of course: her thoughts were too busy with the conversation she'd had with her grandfather the night before.

Maybe he's right, she thought as she made coffee and toast a little later. Maybe I'm not prepared to help hunt a werewolf. As she poured coffee into her cup, though, the other side of the question forced its way to the surface: and if he's hurt or killed when somebody could have been there to help him?

She temporized by going back upstairs and examining her clothes closet with an eye toward the opening day of the museum exhibit. The one garment she owned that seemed suitable was a little black dress of wool crepe she'd picked up two months back at her favorite thrift store in Adocentyn. Looking at it, she realized that it was very nearly the twin of one Audrey

Hepburn had worn in one of the scenes of *Breakfast at Tiffany's*. That amused her, but a glance in her very sparsely populated jewelry box didn't turn up anything that would go with it. She considered that, and decided that a trip to the Ivy Street Thrift Emporium a little later that morning might fix that. The fact that it would also make a good distraction from a choice she didn't want to think about also had a place in her mind as she went back down the stairs.

An hour or so later, after she'd distracted herself with a flurry of chores and made sure her grandfather wouldn't need her for a few hours, she bundled up in her warm coat and headed out into the blustery gray morning. Ivy Street was familiar ground and she didn't think anyone would be following her that morning, but her nerves were on edge; every car on the street and every pedestrian on the sidewalks stood out as though someone had trained a spotlight on each of them. Nobody seemed to be shadowing her, though. She reached the thrift store without incident.

The thrift store had the same genially rundown air as usual. Ariel considered going straight to the glass display case where jewelry and other expensive items were kept, but habit won out; she got a cart, went to the women's clothing section, and spent a quarter hour or so looking at vintage clothing. That day there was nothing in her size she was willing to be caught dead wearing, but the time spent sorting through the latest assortment of gaudy finery and impressively hideous polyester gowns left her feeling a little less frayed than before.

A visit to the shelves that held used books was a little more profitable. Down underneath three full shelves of Bertie Scrubb novels was a row of old paperbacks, and in among them she found a copy of a novel by Hermann Hesse, a writer she'd heard of but hadn't read yet. The title was *Peter Camenzind* and a quick glance inside showed that it was an English translation; she turned a few pages, decided she would probably like it well enough to be worth the dollar it cost, and put it in her cart.

The route from there to the display case took her straight through the middle of the toy section, which meant more Bertie Scrubb to glare at: action figures, mostly, including a cloying little plastic Appaloosa pony who she gathered was supposed to be one of the Pony Pals. She pushed on past, got to the display case and started looking. A pair of pearl earrings caught her eye, and so did a single strand of pearls—those would go well with the black dress, she knew.

Then she went further along the glass case, and saw the silver blade.

It was a letter opener, she realized after a moment, but it had the shape of a medieval dagger and it was almost as large as one. Leaning close over the glass, she could see the words STERLING SILVER stamped onto the blade just in front of the crossguard. She stared at it for a long moment, then turned away sharply and went looking for a clerk.

"The case? Sure," said the first one she found, a middle-aged woman with a fake tan, frizzy black hair and oversized glasses. "Let me get the key. I'll meet you there." Ariel went back to the case and stood waiting, fretful, until the woman reappeared. "Okay," the woman said. "What do you want?"

She got the earrings and the strand, and then asked to see the letter opener. "Sure," the clerk said, and got it out for her. The blade wasn't especially sharp but Ariel guessed it was sharp enough for what she might need to do. The price was more than she wanted to spend, though, and her thoughts tumbled and jangled around each other, pushing one way and another. She handed it back, saying, "I'm going to have to think about this one." The clerk nodded as though it was the most obvious thing in the world and locked up the case again.

Five minutes later she was outside the Ivy Street Thrift Emporium with her purchases tucked safely in her purse, and no clear sense of what to do next. She considered going to Aunt Clarice's shop and asking for a tea leaf reading, but quailed at the thought of explaining her perplexity to the old woman. After a minute or two, as the wind brought salt-scented air whipping past her, she remembered another option.

A brisk walk down the curve of Culpeper Hill brought her to the old waterfront stretched out along the north side of Coopers Bay. Most of a century had passed since the last working ships had tied up there—they were all on the other side of the bay now, where big red cranes rose up stark against the low hills of South Adocentyn—and tourist traps filled the old wooden piers in place of warehouses. That late in the year, even on a Saturday, Harbor Street was nearly empty, and maybe half of the businesses had quietly shut down for the winter, but the one that she needed was still open.

Duplessy's Museum wasn't really a museum. It was a tourist attraction of a traditional variety, with the usual complement of two-headed calves, mummified dogs, optical illusions, and the like. Ariel was prepared to pay the entrance fee, but remembered just as she came in sight of the lurid signs out front that she could get where she needed by way of the lobby. That was empty, and the young black man behind the ticket window looked bored and tired until he noticed her, after which he straightened up and put on a smile. Ariel gave him what she hoped was an apologetic look and crossed the lobby.

The mechanical fortune teller sat next to the exit turnstile, a waist-high box with a tall glass case atop it, and in it a mysterious figure in a hooded robe. Its face was hidden, its gender anyone's guess, and the hand that hovered over a spread of faded tarot cards communicated nothing, but Ariel had consulted it once before and gotten good advice, and she knew from Aunt Clarice that the Hooded One had a reputation as a source of wisdom. She stood in front of it and thought at it: Please help me do the right thing. Then she fished some coins from her purse, set the dials to her birthdate and pulled the lever. The machine duly spat out a slip of paper that read:

> *This is a time when you must face your fears and overcome them. You have some of what you need to do what must be done, but not all. You will face an unwelcome discovery but things will work out in the end. Trust those you know well, follow your intuition, and keep out of sight of enemies. Silver brings you good luck.*

Ariel read that twice, left the lobby, and went out into the blustery air. Wind over Coopers Bay set the waves surging and splashing, but the clouds had begun to break. She walked to the outdoor seating area beside Captain Curdie's Fish & Chips, went over to the railing and looked down at the churning water. That was where she'd dropped the broken halves of her last smartphone into the harbor: a good place for thinking things out and making decisions, she reminded herself, with a little good luck hovering around it as well.

Maybe ten minutes later she left the railing and set out for the nearest street leading up Culpeper Hill. The route she followed was one she knew by heart, up a block to Moon Street and along that narrow and slightly winding thoroughfare to a narrow storefront, where neon tubes in purple and white proclaimed Aunt Clarice's abilities. She braced herself and went through the door into the familiar scents of hot wax and herb-infused oils.

"Good morning, Ariel," Aunt Clarice called out from in back the moment the door closed behind her. "Just a moment and I'll be out."

Ariel went to the counter and waited, and after the predicted moment, the old woman came out from the alcove in back where she did her tea leaf readings. "Good morning," Ariel said. "I hope I'm not interrupting anything. I—I just need to buy some herbs and a bag."

Bright inscrutable eyes gazed up at her. "No, it'll be just under half an hour before my next client comes in. Which herbs?"

"A quarter ounce of fern seed, a quarter ounce of—" It took her a moment to remember the folk name of cinquefoil. "Of five finger grass. And I'm not sure what the third should be."

"You know there ought to be a third," said Aunt Clarice. "Good. Do you know what you need to do?"

"I think so. I got a reading from the Hooded One a few minutes ago."

"Very wise of you. In that case, tell me what you need and I'll tell you what I'd suggest."

"I need not to be seen," Ariel said. "I need to be safe. This is for something dangerous, but as long as nobody notices me, I'll be fine."

"Fern seed and five-finger grass," the old woman said. "Those are good for that sort of work, but if there's real danger you need something a little less subtle. In your place I'd use black mustard seed. That's strong magic, and it can be used for all kinds of bad work, but one thing it'll do for you is confuse people who are trying to see you or find you."

"Thank you," said Ariel. "That's the cat's pajamas."

The outdated slang got her an amused look. "Why don't you go ahead, get the herbs and a bag, and make the toby right here. I want to see how you handle making one when you don't have one of my recipes to work with."

Ariel nodded and went to the glass-fronted cabinet behind the counter where jars of herbs shared space with crystal balls and other expensive magical items. Three jars came out onto the counter, along with a little bag of black cloth, a digital scale, a roll of waxed paper, and a collection of small scoops of various sizes. After two months studying with Aunt Clarice, assembling a toby was nearly second nature for her. She got the herbs measured and mixed, made a little impromptu funnel out of the piece of paper, and poured them neatly into the bag.

"Before you tie that shut," said Aunt Clarice. She'd stooped and extracted two small items from under the counter: a little bottle of dark blue glass and an eyedropper. "One drop of this to give it a blessing. It's something very old and strange you're caught up in, child."

Ariel glanced at her. "You saw that in the tea leaves."

"Of course I did. I don't always see you or Cassie there, but now and again, yes."

The bottle vanished back under the counter, and the eyedropper went into the little bowl where Ariel had learned to put things that needed cleaning. Meanwhile Ariel tied the toby shut, measured and cut the cord to fit around her neck, and put it in a little paper bag to carry home. When she was finished, Aunt Clarice motioned toward the old mechanical cash register, and Ariel grinned, wrote up a receipt for herself, rang up the purchase, paid and gave herself the change. "How's that?" she asked, then: "I can wash up the dropper and the scoops if you want."

"No, you have something else to get and you need to go get it now." She made a shooing motion toward the door. "Besides, that client's going to be here any time now."

"Thank you," Ariel said. "Seriously, thank you."

She was on the sidewalk alongside Moon Street a minute later. Ten minutes of brisk walking, zigzagging east and north by turns, got her back to the Ivy Street Thrift Emporium, and she breathed a sigh of relief when she spotted the silver letter opener still in the glass case. It took her a few minutes to find somebody who could unlock the case and hand her the blade, but the day wasn't much further along when she headed back up Ivy Street with the letter opener tucked into her purse.

Her grandfather was out when she got home, which didn't surprise her greatly. Once she'd put the pearl strand and the earrings in her jewelry box and read the Hooded One's prophecy again, she went downstairs and found the copy of Eliphas

Lévi's *Dogme et Rituel de la Haute Magie*, where she'd read about werewolves two months back. It didn't take long to find the chapter she wanted, and her mastery of French, though still imperfect, was more than adequate to make sense of what Lévi had to say. She shivered more than once reading it, remembering what her grandfather had said about werewolves the night before. The thought that people still knew how to take on an astral wolf-form intrigued her but it also frightened her. The Rev. Sabine Baring-Gould's stories of people torn to pieces by wolf-shapes in the medieval woods murmured through the crawlspaces of her mind.

Nor was it hard for her to imagine at least one person who might be taking on a wolf-shape once the full moon rose. Her conversation on the bus with Kyle Harshaw came surging up to mind, and then the conversation further back with his mother. If Leonora Blake had been a werewolf, as Austin said his grandmother had told him, then it wasn't just young men who learned the trick of transferring consciousness into an astral wolf-form—and if that was true, then Ariel could think all too easily of someone who wanted the plaque badly and might do quite literally anything to get it.

Would Holly Harshaw kill for it, if it came to that? The question hung in the silence, unanswerable.

Ariel got up from the couch and made herself go on to other things. Hours passed. The sun was low in the west, casting a red glow on scattered clouds, before Dr. Moravec got home. Ariel had her purse down with her by the time he came in the door, and waited as usual while he shed his coat, settled on his chair, and sat there with closed eyes for a time. Finally he opened his eyes, considered her, and said, "I gather you've decided you want to assist me tonight."

The words startled her, but only for a moment. "Yes. Yes, I do."

He gave her a long inscrutable look. "You understand that there may be some considerable danger involved. People die now and then in situations like this."

"I know," said Ariel. "I—I got something just in case." She reached into her purse. The letter opener gleamed in lamplight as she brought it out.

He extended a hand. "May I?"

"Sure. It's not consecrated or anything."

He took it, examined it carefully. "Sterling silver. That should be quite adequate. Where did you find it?"

Despite everything, that called up a smile. "My favorite thrift store. You never know what's going to turn up there."

"So I see." He handed it back, and she put it in her purse. "I want to make sure you understand exactly what's involved. If you thrust that into the middle of a projected wolf-form, someone will find a corpse in the morning. Whose the corpse will be is not something you'll have any way of knowing in advance." He said the words in a calm and matter-of-fact tone, which made them all the more troubling.

Ariel closed her eyes and nodded. "I know. Do you think the werewolf will be able to sense the silver, and stay away?"

"The traditional lore doesn't say."

She opened her eyes. "That's not the only thing I have, though." She got out the toby and held it out in her palm.

Her grandfather glanced at it, then at her. "Did Clarice Jackson make that?"

"No. I did."

His eyebrows rose noticeably. "Then you've been putting your studies to good use. That's welcome, though not at all surprising." She blushed; if he noticed he made no sign of it. "If I had to guess, I'd say there were fern spores and cinquefoil in that, and something else I'm not sure I recognize."

"Black mustard seed," said Ariel. "Aunt Clarice suggested that. And a drop of one of her oils, I don't know which one. The rest was my idea."

Dr. Moravec nodded. "Did she advise you more generally?"

"No, not really. Before I went to her shop I went down to the waterfront, to Duplessy's Museum, and asked the Hooded One."

The eyebrows went up again, even further than before. "I wasn't aware that you knew about the Hooded One."

That called up an unwilling smile. "I don't know if you remember, but two days after I got here during the summer I took the tourist bus around town and then went down to the waterfront to see the aquarium and Duplessy's. I remembered those from when I was here back when I was a kid. I spent two quarters on a fortune, and it came true, every word of it."

"That doesn't surprise me in the least."

"Aunt Clarice said once that it's not just an ordinary fortune-telling machine. So I decided to ask it what to do about this." She found the fortune in her purse, handed it to him.

He read it in perfect silence and handed it back. After a moment: "And you're prepared to accept the consequences of following his advice."

His? Ariel filed the pronoun for future reference. "Yeah."

He considered her for another moment, and then nodded. "In that case I'm going to ask you to do something very specific, if you're willing."

"Go ahead."

"It wasn't an accident that you saw the print you did in Culpeper Park. I have very good reason to think that that's where our werewolf will start his activities tonight. If he intends to steal the Faliscan plaque, he'll go west, staying in the shelter of the trees as long as possible, and leave the park at the west end, at Beacon Avenue. I want you to find a place where you can keep watch on that end of the park, and see what happens. I don't suppose Theophilus taught you how to make yourself hard to spot."

"No," said Ariel, "but I've read a little about that, and I've got the toby." She drew in a breath. "I can go watch the west end of the park if you think that's the best thing for me to try."

"Excellent. Dinner, then, and—" His gesture indicated the gathering dusk outside. "A night of werewolf hunting."

CHAPTER *14*

THE NIGHT OF THE SHADOWS

The night air pressed against her, cold and damp, as Ariel followed her grandfather out onto the sidewalk. The sky overhead was a mix of dim clouds and streaks of dark sky speckled with stars, and the wind blew fitfully from the northwest. Pale light spilled onto the sidewalk here and there: moonlight, Ariel realized after a moment, slanting down from low in the east through gaps between the houses. She glanced at her grandfather, waited.

The old man stood gazing toward the park for a few minutes in perfect silence. What he saw there Ariel had no idea, but finally he nodded, turned to her. "You'll want to get in position soon," he said in a low voice. "I don't think there will be much delay. Stay out of sight, and stay downwind if you possibly can." She nodded, put the toby around her neck, and hurried down to the corner of Starr Street, half a block closer to the harbor. There, looking east for a moment, she could see the full moon rising low and golden above the roofs of Adocentyn. She turned her back on it and went on.

Starr Street ran parallel to the edge of Culpeper Park, one block further south. Ariel set out along it, her senses on edge the way they'd been when she'd had her lesson in tradecraft with Theophilus Cray. Her grandfather was probably right, she decided. If a werewolf would shortly roam the city on its way to the Heydonian, it would likely stay in among the trees as long as possible to keep out of sight. At that hour of the night there were still cars on the streets and pedestrians on the sidewalks. That offered some hope that the werewolf wouldn't notice her; the toby she'd gotten from Aunt Clarice offered more; and if worst came to worst, she reminded herself, she had the silver letter opener in her purse.

One block gave way to another. The night grew quieter and the moon rose further. Ariel hurried on. By the time she got to Beacon Avenue, which cut at an angle across the neatly platted streets and avenues of the Culpeper Hill neighborhood, she needed to stop and catch her breath. Fortunately she could see the west end of the park clearly from there. Well lit by streetlights, it started a little more than a block away and ran for four more blocks. An unpruned hedge surrounding a big half-timbered house on the corner of Starr and Beacon gave her a hiding place of sorts. She stood just behind the corner of the hedge, her heart drumming, half of her hoping that nothing would happen and the other half irrationally certain that sometime soon a lean gray shape would come loping out from under the trees.

Time passed, and the flow of cars dwindled. She began to wonder if she was on a fool's errand, waiting for something that wouldn't appear. Then, as a gap in the traffic left Beacon Avenue clear of cars for more than a block either way, the shape she half expected came out from the trees. It was black, not gray, and not quite opaque—she could see lights and shadows faintly through it—but it looked and moved like a timber wolf, and it trotted across the street without a moment's hesitation.

She was about to move when something else caught her eye, a little behind the wolf. A second wolf-shape came trotting behind, a little more diffidently. It was gray rather than black, and didn't look quite as solid as the first one. A moment passed before Ariel realized that neither of the wolf-shapes cast a shadow.

Another moment passed as she stared and tried to convince herself she wasn't frightened. During that moment, she considered staying there and seeing how long it took the two wolves to return; she considered hurrying back as fast as she could run to the house on Lyon Avenue; but she discarded both those options, and made herself follow the wolves. Her heart pounded and her knees didn't feel as steady as she liked, but she knew the street they seemed to be heading along, Warder Street, and remembered that it ran straight to the Heydonian. That realization sent her across Beacon Avenue to a parallel street, and made her hurry along it. She reached into her purse, found the letter opener by feel, and got it out. The metal felt cold in her hand. She gripped it tight and hoped it wouldn't be needed.

The street she followed brought her at last to an old mansion across from the Heydonian, sheltering behind a brick wall. She scurried to the corner of the wall, crouched down a little and looked around it, just as two low dark shapes darted across the street a block further on. The two werewolves stopped on the sidewalk in front of one of the Heydonian's blank walls, heads together as though conferring. Then the black one, who seemed to be leading the other, trotted straight toward the wall and vanished into it as though it was no more substantial than a fogbank. The second followed a little more slowly, and vanished in its turn.

Ariel shivered, feeling a chill the night wind didn't explain. With an effort, she pushed the sudden uprush of dread aside and got her mind clear enough to function. The Heydonian library was open until midnight, she thought she remembered, but the museum would have closed hours before, and—yes, what was on the other side of the wall the werewolves had gone through was one end of the museum. She could imagine easily enough the dimly lit rooms with their treasures, the werewolves moving through the shadows, heading for the new exhibit and the carnelian moon in its bronze plaque.

No doubt one of them could grip it in wolf-jaws and pry it loose from the wall. Once that happened—

She blinked, and had to stifle a sudden laugh. Wolf-forms condensed from the astral light could pass through most material objects at will, that was what the books said, but bronze and carnelian weren't so flexible. The werewolves could get the plaque down from the wall, but how could they get it out of the museum through locked doors and marble walls?

Ariel's imagination promptly served up images of window glass shattering and a wolf-shape leaping down to the sidewalk. Nothing like that happened. She stayed where she was, crouching behind the corner of the brick wall, as motionless as tired muscles and trembling nerves would allow. Minutes passed and the full moon rose further. Then, all at once, the two wolf-shapes came side by side through the Heydonian's marble wall and set off the way they had come. Neither of them held anything visible clutched in its jaws.

That was as much as Ariel needed to see. She turned and hurried back along the street, breaking into a run. Winded again, she stopped at Beacon Avenue, found a place behind an ornamental shrub where she could crouch and keep watch. A minute or so passed. Cars moved up and down the avenue, passing in and out of pools of light beneath the streetlamps. Then another long gap in the traffic opened up, and two dark shapes that cast no shadows loped across the street and vanished beneath the trees of Culpeper Park.

She stayed there for another minute or so before she went to the crosswalk, waited for the light, and started for home at a less frantic pace. Her nerves were still on edge. She started to put the silver letter opener back in her purse, then changed her mind. Careful though she'd been, she knew the werewolves might have seen her or scented her—and it was just possible that they might already know who she was and where she lived. She walked on, eyes and ears alert. Two blocks passed without incident.

Then she heard a faint quiet rhythmic sound ahead of her.

She slowed, listened. The night had grown still, and in the silence she could hear the sounds from the cross street ahead, low but getting louder. She stopped, listened more closely. Something was coming down the street from the park, something that made a faint uneven rattling sound with each step. A moment passed before she was sure it sounded like a dog pacing, its footfalls soft but its claws striking the concrete. Another moment and she was certain there were two of them, their paws striking slightly different rhythms.

A quick frantic look around showed no place to hide, just dark houses pressed up close to the sidewalk on both sides. She clutched the silver letter opener with frantic strength, braced herself, and wondered whether someone would find her body there on the street the next morning—or whether another corpse or two would turn up somewhere else.

Then a big brown and black Airedale on a leash came into sight in the pool of light under the corner streetlamp. Another followed it. Both of them cast black shadows on the sidewalk. The two dogs started across the street, straining at the leashes. Behind them came a plump middle-aged man in a long coat and a driving cap, holding the leashes in one hand and puffing on a cigarette he held in the other. They crossed the street and kept going, and the clicking of claws on concrete and the whisper of the man's footfalls faded promptly. None of them appeared to notice Ariel at all.

Ariel sagged with relief and embarrassment, made herself go onward. No other sounds came to her ears but the ordinary noises of a quiet Adocentyn night. She got to Lyon Avenue without incident, saw her grandfather standing outside the front door of the house, took off the toby and all but ran toward him.

"Did you see them?" he asked at once.

She nodded. Before she could go on, he motioned to the door and let them both in. Only after they were inside did she glance up at him sharply and say, "You knew there was more than one of them."

"Of course." He got his coat settled on the coat tree. "There were two, one old and experienced, one quite a bit younger and, I think, relatively new to lycanthropy. The older one's wolf form was black, the younger one gray."

"You saw the wolves too."

"No." He turned toward the parlor. "I trust a cup of tea will be welcome."

She gave him a baffled look, but managed to say "Yes."

He went toward the kitchen as she got her coat and shoulder bag settled in their places. By the time she followed him he had the kettle going and was on his way to his usual chair. "So," he said. "I want you to tell me exactly what you did and what you saw."

"Sure." Ariel curled up on her corner of the couch, drew in a deep unsteady breath, and described everything she'd witnessed. The whole time she spoke, Dr. Moravec sat listening with his usual calm expression on his face, saying nothing, reacting to nothing. When she finished, he nodded, and for a moment she was sure he would remain silent, but the moment passed and he said, "Thank you. That plus what I witnessed myself gives me nearly every piece of information I need to finish solving this case. That said—" He leaned forward a little. "You put yourself in quite some danger by following them, and I don't think that was wise."

"I know." She shrugged. "But I thought it was worth doing."

The old man considered her for a moment, and then nodded. "Very well. You have the right to make your own decisions, of course."

"Thank you," said Ariel. "I know I'm not very experienced at this stuff yet—"

"But you're not a child anymore."

Her smile was a little unsteady. "Thank you."

The kettle squalled in the kitchen. Ariel got to her feet before her grandfather could start to rise, fixed the tea and brought it back into the parlor. A little while passed. She sipped tea, and then asked, "So how did you know about the werewolves?"

"Because I found their human bodies in the park."

Ariel blinked in surprise, opened her mouth to ask the obvious question, then closed it.

"You'll know the details soon enough," he went on. "There were two of them, as I said, hidden neatly in a hollow place under bushes toward the middle of the park, in very deep trance. Stark naked, by the way, with their clothes folded neatly beside them, just as the old books said; it was apparently required by some traditions of lycanthropy to create the astral form outdoors, in the light of the full moon. Each one wore a belt that I'm fairly sure was wolfskin, with the fur still on it, one black, one gray. The belts had buckles with nine tongues, just as the old records said. They must have used some kind of magical salve on their skin—I could smell some of the herbs. They also used a standard bit of European folk magic to keep passersby from noticing them lying there, a classic invisibility spell. It was capably done, but—" He allowed a shrug. "There are very few spells of that kind I can't see past, and I've trained myself to notice their presence. So I was able to locate them without too much difficulty."

Ariel took that in. "What did you do?"

"I left a note for each of them pinned to their clothing, explaining that I knew who they were and what they were doing, and requesting both of them to come to a certain conference room at the Heydonian at nine o'clock tomorrow morning. I didn't sign the notes, of course. If I had, it's not impossible that they might try to break into this house and kill me tonight."

That possibility hadn't occurred to Ariel, and it sent a cold shudder down her back. "Do you think they might be able to find out who left the notes anyway?"

"It's possible," he admitted. "I included something in the note to encourage them not to make the attempt." He reached into one of his pockets, pulled out a small automatic pistol. Ariel blinked, then stared.

"One of my fellow trustees," he said then, "is a gun collector with a great many unusual weapons in his collection. He's quite skilled at making exotic ammunition for the stranger guns he owns, and so it was a very easy thing to have him make a few dozen very special rounds for this pistol. I don't imagine I have to tell you what kind they are."

"Silver bullets," she said, suppressing a shudder.

"Exactly. I've placed certain protective spells around this house that will make it difficult for anything to get in. If the werewolves manage to get past that, I have my pistol. If they decide to break into the house in their ordinary material bodies, the alarm system will bring the police, and if worst comes to worst, silver bullets are just as dangerous to material bodies."

He learned forward. "I won't be sleeping tonight. You should sleep if you can, but please keep your silver knife by your bedside. If you hear gunfire or the alarm goes off, stay in your room, turn on a light, and keep the knife in your hand until I come up to tell you that it's safe—or until the police arrive and do the same thing."

"Okay," she said after a moment of frozen silence. Then: "So what happens now?"

"I call the Heydonian's security office and have them check the museum—especially the Faliscan plaque. If it's missing, as I expect, the museum will be locked down immediately, but only a very few people will be informed of that. You're right that the werewolves couldn't take the plaque with them, so it will be hidden somewhere inside the Heydonian, and the hiding place will be somewhere that a werewolf can reach without passing through anything solid. So the thieves, or one of them at least, will have to return for it. Since they have to minimize the risk that the plaque will be found by security, my guess is that one of them will visit the museum sometime very soon, probably using the same invisibility spell, and make off with the plaque before anyone notices anything." He allowed a faint cold smile. "The thieves' plan was clever enough, all things considered. But there are two things they don't know. No, three."

Ariel gave him an uncertain look. "Go on."

He held up one finger. "First, I've instructed the security office to check the new exhibit every morning before opening, so even if we hadn't spotted the werewolves, the theft would have come to light too soon for the thieves' convenience." Another finger rose. "Second, we did spot the werewolves, you tracked them to the Heydonian and back, and so we have a good ten hours or so of additional warning. And third—" He raised a third finger, then stopped. "No, that's a surprise I mean to keep to myself for the moment. I think you'll find it very amusing."

"You've done some magic?"

Dr. Moravec shook his head. "No, sometimes the best way to deal with a situation like this is on the material plane. It will help if you bring your camera. Color film, please."

She gave him a puzzled look, which he met with his usual bland expression. "Oh, and you'll want to get as much sleep as you can. Tomorrow will be a very busy day."

CHAPTER 15

A BLAZE OF CRIMSON

That night's practice with the shewstone brought Ariel nothing but a frayed temper, as she couldn't keep her mind off the werewolves and her grandfather's words for more than a few moments at a time. Once she finished getting ready for bed and settled underneath the covers, she tried to make herself relax, then realized she'd forgotten to put the silver letter opener on her bedside table and made herself go get it. That set a cascade of worries and stark terrors running through her mind, and for a while she was sure she wouldn't sleep at all that night.

Sleep came finally, though, and brought vague formless dreams in which dim shapes she could never quite see moved through a deeper darkness. Then, when the first gray light was trickling through the curtains, Dr. Moravec woke her with a crisp knock on her door. "Time to get ready," he said through the door. "We need to be at the Heydonian in an hour." Ariel scrambled out of bed, got showered and dressed as quickly as she could, and wasted five minutes doing her breathing exercise and five more staring at the crystal while distracting thoughts jabbered at her.

Once that was done, she had just enough time to make and eat some toast, gulp down a cup of coffee, and make sure her camera and her investigation bag were ready for the day, before it was time to follow her grandfather out into the cold air of early morning and climb into the old Buick. As the engine warmed up, she asked, "So what happened?"

"I called security last night," said Dr. Moravec. "They told me that the plaque was still in its place on the wall."

Ariel sent an astonished look his way. "What?"

"That was a possibility I'd prepared for. I called Terry O'Shaughnessy and told him, and he called me back fifteen minutes later. The plaque on the wall is a modern replica. It looks very like the original, but if you put it under a microscope—" He eased the car out into the street, headed for the Heydonian. "The marks left by modern machine tools are distinctive. It's child's play to tell them apart from the marks left by Iron Age hand tools. Terry took magnified photographs of the original as soon as we received it from the Harshaw estate, and it was just as easy to compare those to the replica and prove that the two weren't the same."

"That," said Ariel, "is the cat's pajamas. Seriously."

"There are tricks worth knowing in this business," said her grandfather. "So we know that the plaque was stolen, and we know that it's somewhere in the Heydonian building, probably in the museum itself, quite possibly wherever the replica was hidden—the werewolves didn't bring it in with them, after all. Terry knows what to do to find it. I expect to have good news by the time we arrive. Still, we'll see."

Lights gleamed in windows to either side of the street. A pale gray dawn spread over Adocentyn. A few more blocks slid past, the rising sun splashed red light across the clouds overhead, and then the Buick nosed into an empty parking place across the street from the Heydonian. Traffic was sparse and they didn't have to wait to cross the street and go through the big bronze door into the entrance hall. Empty and silent, the great soaring space took the sound of their footfalls and turned them into uneasy whispers.

A stocky middle-aged woman in a plain gray jacket and black slacks stood next to the museum door. "Good morning, Dr. Moravec," she said as the two of them approached.

"Good morning, Deirdre. Anything?"

"Dr. O'Shaughnessy's already in, and two of my staff."

"Of course. For the record, this is my granddaughter Ariel."

"Pleased to meet you," the woman said. "Deirdre McTavish, assistant head of security here." She took Ariel's hand in a quick professional grip. To Dr. Moravec: "I'll let them know."

She got a cell phone out of one pocket, tapped on it three times, and said, "Peter? Dr. Moravec and Ms. Ariel Moravec." Someone apparently answered, and she pocketed the phone, unlocked the museum door, and let them in.

Inside the lights were still mostly off. The lobby was an empty space in near-darkness. Once they went beyond it, statues and glass cases loomed up like phantasms. Most of them were unknown to Ariel, but she spotted the replica of the Kynokefale machine quickly enough: on a low pedestal, its dials facing the ceiling, the open end she could see full of shadows. As they neared the one room that was brightly lit, Dr. O'Shaughnessy came out to meet them.

"We used the lamp," said Dr. O'Shaughnessy once greetings were done with. "You were quite correct, of course. I had Baynes take the photos you asked for."

"Thank you. And the plaque?"

"Located. Quite an ingenious hiding place. Care to guess?" Dr. Moravec gave him a bland tolerant look, and he chuckled and said, "Inside the replica of the Kynokefale machine, down underneath the gears where a metal detector wouldn't find it. Very clever. Of course your little trick made it shine like a traffic light. There was a fine set of tracks, too."

Ariel gave her grandfather an uncertain look, but he simply nodded.

"Do you want the plaque for the next part of this?" Dr. O'Shaughnessy asked then.

"The duplicate will be quite sufficient."

That got him a brusque nod from Dr. O'Shaughnessy. "That seems sensible. Where do you want it?"

"Conference Room 3. I expect the perpetrators to show up there in a quarter hour."

Bushy white eyebrows went up in response. "If you can make that happen, Bernard, I'll be impressed."

Dr. Moravec nodded. "I'd like you to be present, if that's an option. Another witness would be useful."

"I'll be there."

Dr. Moravec nodded again, and turned to go. Ariel gave him a dubious glance, but followed him back out of the museum.

The conference rooms were further back in the building, off the entrance hall through an unobtrusive door of wood and glass near the main elevator. Dr. Moravec led the way to Conference Room 3, a quiet little space with a bland oval Danish-modern table in the middle, half a dozen equally anonymous chairs around it, and a little counter along part of one wall that featured a coffee maker and a dozen or so plain white cups. To Ariel's surprise, the coffee pot was full and steaming. In another corner of the room, an unshaded lamp rose up on a stark metal lampstand. The bulb was an odd purple color.

Dr. Moravec gestured at the coffee pot. "Help yourself. I trust you won't mind pouring coffee for our guests."

"Nope," Ariel said, and filled herself a cup. "You?"

"Not yet, thank you." He sat on the side of the table furthest from the door, gestured toward the narrow end closest to the counter and the coffee. "If you could sit there, that would be best. I'll need you to describe exactly what you saw last night, when I give the signal. Have your camera ready, but out of sight. It has a flash? Excellent. You'll know what to photograph once it appears. Take several pictures as quickly as possible."

Ariel, baffled, nodded but settled onto the chair he'd indicated. Her shoulder bag went into the chair next to her, open, with the camera on top of the other contents. Below it, the silver letter opener glinted, catching the light.

Minutes passed. Ariel sipped coffee and tried not to let herself get any more nervous than she already was. When a muffled sound from outside the room told of a door opening, though, she jumped a little, and blushed pointlessly. Dr. Moravec glanced at her, turned his gaze back toward nothing in particular.

Then the door opened, and Dr. O'Shaughnessy came in. "It's all seen to," he said. "A very fine collection of footprints, by the bye, and rather a mess on the wall."

"Good." Dr. Moravec motioned to a chair next to his. "The plaque can go on the table."

"Certainly." A bronze plaque Ariel couldn't tell apart from the one in the display found its way onto the center of the table. Dr. O'Shaughnessy went around the table and sat.

Dr. Moravec handed him a little black device that looked like the remote control for a television. "Here you are. Any questions?"

"None in the world."

"Coffee?" Ariel asked him after the briefest of pauses.

"Please. Cream and sugar, if you don't mind." Ariel poured him a cup, found him the creamer and the sugar packets, and went back to her chair.

Another silence passed. Then the door to the entrance hall opened again, a little more tentatively. A pause, and then the door to the conference room followed suit, admitting Gerard Breyer. That startled Ariel, but only for a moment, as the pieces to the puzzle began one by one to fall into place.

"Ah," said Breyer, with a slight smile, taking in the plaque on the table and the three people seated around it. "I see I underestimated you, Dr. Moravec. Perhaps you can introduce me to your colleague."

"Dr. Terence O'Shaughnessy, our director of research. Terry, this is Gerard Breyer." Dr. Moravec gestured at the side of the table closest to the door. "Please have a seat. Coffee?"

Breyer nodded after a moment. "Please. Black, if you will." Ariel got up, poured him a cup, and brought it to him. He gave her a quizzical glance, but thanked her.

"I trust," said Dr. Moravec then, "that your companion will be with us shortly."

Breyer had begun to lift his cup, but set it down. "I'd prefer to leave my apprentice out of this. The entire project was my idea, and I don't want him to suffer any penalty when he was guilty of nothing worse than loyalty to his teacher."

"I understand," said Dr. Moravec, "but I must insist on speaking to both of you. There are potential legal charges involved, as I trust you realize. Since the plaque never left the premises of the museum, the Heydonian would prefer not to press charges, but—" The old man shrugged. "If it's necessary, we can do that."

"Seriously?" said Breyer. "I hardly think that charges of lycanthropy would be heard by any court in this day and age."

Dr. Moravec smiled and said nothing. After a long moment, Breyer sighed and nodded. "Very well. He's not far away, as I gather you're aware."

"It seemed likely," said Dr. Moravec.

Breyer got a cell phone out from an inside pocket of his jacket, sent a text, waited a moment, and then said, "He's on his way. He expects to be here in just a few minutes."

"Thank you," said Dr. Moravec.

The cell phone went away. "I trust you'll forgive my curiosity," said Breyer then, "how you connected me and my apprentice to the business concerning the plaque."

Dr. Moravec glanced at Ariel, who said, "A little after eleven o'clock last night, Mr. Breyer, I watched two shapes that looked a lot like wolves leaving the west end of Culpeper Park, where it ends at Beacon Avenue. One of the shapes was black, the other was gray, and neither one cast a shadow. The black one went ahead and the gray one followed. They crossed Beacon Avenue during a break in the traffic, followed Warder Street all the way to the Heydonian, and went right through the wall of the building. They came back out around fifteen minutes later and went the same way back to the park.

That's where I lost sight of them. I think we both know who one of those wolves was."

Breyer was staring at her with narrowed eyes by the time she finished. He looked, she thought, uncomfortably like a wolf just then. "I find it very hard to believe that anyone could have followed us without being seen or scented."

"There was magic involved," Ariel admitted.

His gaze didn't waver at all. "You must have been confident in it. Facing us isn't a risk most people take."

In answer, she reached into her purse, brought out the silver letter opener, and set it on the table without a word.

He drew back suddenly. "I see." After an uncomfortable pause: "In that case, I—" He stopped in mid-sentence, and an instant later Ariel realized why: someone had opened the door onto the entrance hall.

In the moment following that soft sound, as she put the letter opener back in her purse, an appalling possibility surfaced in Ariel's mind. Maybe it was the rhythm of the footsteps she heard faintly, maybe something else, but she suddenly guessed who would come through the door. Before she could do more than register it, the door to the conference room opened, and the possibility became real as Austin Wronski stepped into the room.

She managed to keep her reaction to herself, but Austin glanced around and saw her, and his face stiffened. Breyer motioned him to a chair, and he sat. "I don't believe we've met," said Dr. Moravec. "I'm Dr. Bernard Moravec and this is Dr. Terence O'Shaughnessy."

"Austin Wronski."

"Coffee?"

"No, thank you."

Dr. Moravec nodded, and turned to Dr. O'Shaughnessy. "Now."

A quiet click was the only response. An instant later the odd light fixture in the corner turned on, casting a diffuse purple glow over everything—and in response, vivid scarlet light flared into being on Breyer's and Austin's hands, and on the lower half of Austin's face.

Stunned though she was, Ariel knew what she had to do. The camera came up as though it was pulling her hands with it. The first flash lit up the room, sending stark shadows against the walls, and startled everyone there but Dr. Moravec. Second, third, and fourth flashes followed as quickly as the film winder could do its job. She lowered the camera then, tried not to notice the shocked look on Austin's face or the white fury on Breyer's.

"So," Breyer said. All at once he was on his feet, hands clenched. "This was a trap."

"Please sit down," said Dr. Moravec, his calm unbroken. "I meant what I said about avoiding legal charges."

"And this?" Breyer gestured with his glowing hands.

"A guarantee of good behavior," Dr. Moravec said. "We have photographs and witnesses showing dye on the plaque—the real one, not the replica you left in its place—and dye on your hands. That's quite enough to put both of you in prison for two to five years for attempted grand larceny, with no reference to lycanthropy involved. I repeat that we have no intention of pressing charges, so long as neither of you make any further attempt to steal the plaque."

Breyer considered that, sat down. Austin gave him a worried look but said nothing.

"Be grateful," Dr. O'Shaughnessy said then, and turned off the light fixture. The crimson glow vanished instantly. "It's been eight years now since someone last stole something valuable from the Heydonian collections, and she's still in prison."

"I assume," Breyer said bitterly, "there's a price for this special treatment."

"None," said Dr. Moravec. "Other than the detail I specified."

Breyer considered him for a moment. "Why?"

Dr. O'Shaughnessy answered him. "Because you've inherited a rare and ancient tradition. If it still survives anywhere else at all we've never heard of it. It's the mission of the Heydonian to preserve such things."

"That tradition isn't something I can tell you about," said Breyer, "if that's what you're hinting at. Not a word, except under certain very precise conditions. If that means I go to prison, so be it."

"Unnecessary," said Dr. O'Shaughnessy. "That sort of requirement's hardly uncommon. Any questions you can answer, why, quite a few people would be eager to listen, but that hasn't any bearing on this business."

Breyer glanced at Austin, whose look in return said more clearly than words, "Your call." A pause, then Breyer nodded. "Very well," he said. "We'll have to accept, of course. I don't suppose it will do any good to say that the plaque's a sacred object and not for public display."

"Ah," said Dr. Moravec. "So that's why you didn't try to get it from its former owner."

"I considered that," said Breyer. "But he kept it in a safe-deposit box. Bank robbery is a little beyond my skill set."

"Understandably," Dr. Moravec said. "If you can prepare a written description of how the plaque should be handled, I can submit that to the board of trustees. We have quite a few magically charged items in our collections, as I'm sure you're aware, and we make a point of treating them in a proper manner. That's simply a matter of safety." He motioned at the plaque on the table, allowed a smile. "Besides, you've provided us with a very fine replica, which I suspect will be just as suitable for the public to look at."

Breyer considered him for a long moment, and then nodded. "Very well. Yes, I can get you the traditional lore on that subject, or what's known of it. It may be a few days, because I'll have to contact certain people abroad."

Dr. O'Shaughnessy's expression brightened. "So the tradition's survived elsewhere. That's very good to hear."

"A few people in Italy and a few in France," said Breyer. "There are supposed to be other lineages in central and eastern Europe but nobody I know is in contact with them. There haven't been many of us for a very long time." He picked up his coffee, drank some. "I do have one question, if I might ask."

"By all means," said Dr. Moravec.

"How on earth did you get the dye onto the two of us?"

Dr. Moravec allowed a fractional smile. "Yes, I thought that would be a surprise. The medieval accounts insist that the blood of a werewolf's victims could be found on the werewolf's human mouth the next morning, and mud from his travels on his hands and feet. It seemed likely that any other tolerably sticky substance would adhere just as well. So I arranged to have an odorless and transparent fluorescent dye sprayed on the plaque, the wall around it, and the floor under it. You'll be interested to know that the two of you left a very clear set of pawprints from the room where you took the plaque to the Kynokefale machine replica, and from there to the wall you passed through. Some of the dye stuck to the wall, but I gambled that enough would adhere to the astral forms to get back to your physical bodies. As you see, I was correct."

"Very clever."

"Thank you."

"If I were to ask you how to remove the dye, would you tell me?"

"The slow way involves repeated washing with soap, and vinegar rinses."

"And the fast way," Breyer said, "is doubtless one of your professional secrets." He glanced at Dr. Moravec and Dr. O'Shaughnessy. "Well. If there's anything else we need to discuss, I'm all ears."

"To the best of my knowledge," said Dr. Moravec, "that settles the entire business."

"There's one detail remaining." Breyer got to his feet. "I hired you to solve a certain mystery, and you solved it. However inconvenient the solution turned out to be for me, I pay my debts. You'll please submit a bill for your services."

"I'll have it on its way to you later today."

"Thank you. Austin, if you're ready?"

Austin extracted himself from his chair. His face was rigid and he refused to look at Ariel. The door opened, and then closed behind them.

Chapter 16

A TELLTALE MARK

In the moments that followed Ariel forced her thoughts to silence. She understood clearly enough what Austin's presence in the room meant, but she didn't want to have to face that hard reality just yet. She made herself draw in a breath and let it out again, tried to convince herself that the breath wasn't as ragged as it felt.

"Elegantly done," said Dr. O'Shaughnessy. "Miss Moravec, I include you in that. The two of them very nearly jumped out of their skins when that first flash went off." With a wry smile: "*Versipelli* in a slightly different sense, I suppose." He turned to Dr. Moravec. "Anything else? No? I'll take the replica down to the museum and have them put it up in place of the original. I trust that dye of yours won't damage bronze."

"It's safe on every metal I know of," said Dr. Moravec, "though it dissolves nylon and a few other synthetic fibers."

"I'll warn the staff." He hauled himself out of his chair. "Well. No rest for the wicked, and all that." The replica went into one of his jacket pockets, and he headed for the door.

Once he was gone, Dr. Moravec turned to Ariel. "Thank you. I have to agree with Terry—that was very well done. How soon can the film be developed?"

Ariel fought her way back to clarity. "We could drop it off at the camera store on the way home if you want," she said, "and get it tomorrow. There's nothing else on the roll, but—" She forced a smile. "I can afford some more film."

He nodded, and got to his feet. Ariel stood a moment later and followed him to the door. The entrance hall of the Heydonian was almost empty, but she was horrified to realize that "almost" didn't exclude the one person in the world she least wanted to see just then. There he was, waiting beside the big allegorical painting, his lean face pale, intent, visibly nervous.

"Ariel," Austin said, as she came close. "Can you spare a minute?"

Dr. Moravec glanced at the two of them and said to Ariel, "I'll be in the car." He went on to the big bronze door.

Face to face with Austin, Ariel tried to say something and failed. The initial shock had faded, but what it left behind wasn't any of the feelings she expected. Instead, she felt a bleak gray emptiness that seemed to stretch out to the edges of forever.

"I wanted to ask," he said, "if we can get together and talk sometime soon."

The words jabbed hard enough at her failed daydreams that a flicker of anger forced its way through the numbness. "Why? Does Mr. Breyer need to know something else?"

He flinched as though she'd struck him. "No."

"Tell me why I should believe you." Please, she wanted to say. Give me some reason to trust you.

He met her gaze, but his face had gone paler still, and hard. "You can just say no," he said. "You don't have to get nasty about it."

The empty numb feeling tore open, and what was beneath it was anger. "Look," Ariel snapped. "If you cozy up to someone and all you want is to get information out of her, don't be surprised if she decides you're a complete jerk. Okay? Now leave me alone. I don't want to see you ever again."

She pushed past him and stalked away toward the door. The whole way she could feel his gaze on her. The whole way, too, part of her wanted to burst into tears, turn back, apologize. Maybe it was self-respect that kept her from doing that and maybe it was wounded pride, but she kept going.

The bronze door swung open, closed behind her with a heavy hollow clang. Then she was outside in the cold morning air, crossing the sidewalk to the street. The long black car waited on the other side. The whole way she wondered if Austin would come out the door after her, and she felt half relieved and half disappointed when he didn't.

She crossed the street, saw that her grandfather was in the passenger seat of the car, veered over to the door on the driver's side and got in. She fastened the seatbelt, got the engine started, did her best not to pay attention to her grandfather's cool unreadable gaze.

"That was the young man you've been meeting," he said.

Defeated, she let out a sigh, looked at him. "Yeah."

"Did he learn about the plaque from you?"

"No. He told me about it. He said somebody at the museum mentioned it to his mom." She looked away again. "I don't think I told him anything I shouldn't have, but I don't know."

Dr. Moravec nodded. "Well. Fortunately it all turned out for the best."

For the best? Ariel had to choke back a sudden rush of anger and misery. She nodded, put the car in gear and pulled away from the curb.

"One detail I'm still not certain of," he said then, "is exactly how Breyer got the replica into the museum. My guess, though it's only a guess, is that he used the same invisibility spell that he placed around his body and Wronski's last night. It would have been easy enough to slip into the exhibit while workmen were coming and going, and pause by the Kynokefale machine just long enough to put it inside. He could have extracted it the same way once the exhibit was open. I considered having him followed once I was sure he was responsible for all this."

"You knew it was Breyer," she said.

"I knew there was something false about his story the moment I read his letter. He was careful to put the sightings on the days of the full moon but he wasn't quite careful enough with the times. On several of those occasions, the moon was just over the horizon when he claimed to have seen his phantom dog. It takes time for a werewolf to prepare for the ritual, create the wolf-form, and transfer consciousness to it, and none of that can be done until the moon is visible. So the question all along was what kind of game he was playing, and you and Stacy Kretzler, of all people, helped me find the answer to that."

"I'm glad," Ariel said, though she didn't feel glad at all. Her grandfather's glance left her certain that he'd heard everything she hadn't said, and she fixed her attention on the street ahead and kept driving.

The visit to the camera shop took only a few minutes, and most of that went into trying to attend to Bill Kotzebue's ebullient chatter. The relative quiet inside the Buick, once she'd handed over the roll of film for next-day developing and bought two more rolls of black and white for nature images, felt like a sanctuary. The house on Lyon Avenue offered her a deeper solace, woven of silence and familiarity. She shed her coat, considered her options, and said, "Anything I need to do?"

"Nothing I know of," said her grandfather.

"Then I'm going to go lay down for a while. I didn't sleep that well last night."

"I imagine not." He made a shooing motion toward the stair. She didn't have to force the smile she sent him in answer. The steps creaked and sighed beneath her as she went up the stair to the familiar quiet of her room.

She didn't intend to sleep. All she wanted was privacy, silence, and the chance to let herself feel miserable: to cry into her pillow if she needed to, without anyone else knowing about it. Once she kicked off her shoes and flopped on the bed, though, a sudden wave of tiredness broke over her. She blinked, tried to remember what she'd wanted to think about, and then sank into a leaden sleep.

Later, she dreamed. She was sitting in the parlor of an apartment she didn't recognize, curled up in one corner of a sofa while rain hammered on a window nearby. A wrinkled old woman she didn't recognize either, dressed in a dark green dress and a dark gray cardigan, sat on the other end of the sofa facing her. Between them, on the sofa's middle cushion, was a shape Ariel recognized at once: five-sided, the red carnelian disk in the middle flanked by the two wolves, the strange script beneath it.

In the dream, the old woman turned the plaque over and tapped one bony finger on the back. Ariel waited breathlessly, because that gesture meant the little apartment would soon be full of wolves. The wolves didn't appear, though. After a moment she looked at the old woman and tried to ask her why, but the old woman herself had become a wolf. Instead of answering Ariel she smiled, showing long white teeth and a lolling tongue, and tapped again on the back of the plaque with one gray paw.

Then Ariel was blinking awake in her room. The rain she'd heard in her dream was there in the waking world, too, tapping at her window in little flurries as the wind flung it. From the failing light, she'd slept through the middle hours of the day and afternoon was drawing on. She sat up slowly. Fragments of the dream hovered around her in the dim light. They clustered around the same uncomfortable feeling she'd had earlier, the sense that she'd failed to notice something that mattered very much. The familiar furnishings of her room didn't offer any hints, and after a moment she got up and went downstairs.

The house was even more silent than usual, and a note on the kitchen table explained why: *Ariel—I've been called in to the*

Heydonian. Should be back before dinner. She read it, got the teakettle going, and went back into the parlor. Not even the grinning gaze of the little wooden crocodile on top of the bookshelf succeeded in chasing off the feeling that something was very wrong. She looked around the parlor, tried to figure out what the feeling might be hinting at, and finally let out a frustrated sigh and settled on the sofa to wait for the water to boil.

The Carnelian Moon sat waiting on the end table. Just then, she'd gladly have read anything else, but it was the only book in reach and she couldn't find even the slight enthusiasm she'd need to go get something else. She picked it up listlessly, let it fall open. It was typical of the day, she decided, that the pages inevitably gaped open to the black and white photos of the Faliscan plaque. She glanced at the caption, then read it again more closely. Her eyebrows drew together, hard. Then she noticed a tiny detail in one of the photos, and her hand went to her mouth as she realized what it implied.

Abruptly she realized that the teakettle was yelling at her. She flung herself off the sofa, got her tea, came back. The photo and the caption still told her the same thing. She put the teacup down, went up to her room, considered the shelf of old mystery novels she'd collected. The thought of barricading herself in her room and hiding from the thing she'd just realized had its appeal, but she made herself pull out a volume—one of the bleak hardboiled mysteries from late in Raymond Chandler's career, full of lies and betrayals—and went back downstairs with it to the sofa and her cup of tea.

She'd finished that cup and was making another when the front door rattled, announcing Dr. Moravec's return. Guessing at his mood from the sounds in the entry, she found a teapot and cups and got the tea steeping, then put them on a tray and went out into the parlor, bracing herself for the conversation she knew she needed to start. His expression made her falter. She'd lived in his house long enough to begin to see past the inscrutable surface of his expression to catch hints of what lay beneath it, and hints of tension in the corners of his mouth and the space between his eyebrows told her that he'd had unpleasant news.

He glanced toward her as she came out of the kitchen, sent a fractional smile her way. "Thank you. Yes, a cup of tea would be very welcome just now." He settled in his chair as she set the tray on the coffee table. Tea splashed into both cups. Then he considered her and said, "Something's wrong, isn't it?"

Ariel allowed a little tired laugh. "Yeah. I was about to ask you the same thing."

He motioned to her to go on. She got the copy of *The Carnelian Moon*, opened it to the photo of the plaque, turned to the next page and handed it to him. "Read the caption," she said. "Notice what it says about who owned the plaque in 1938."

She watched his eyes move back and forth as he read it, saw the sudden narrowing that told her he'd found the detail that mattered. "Collection of Jacques Hirschberg, Lyon," he said, confirming it. "And of course that's not in the official provenance of the piece."

"Yeah. Now look at the photo of the back."

He did, then glanced up at her. "And?"

"See the little paper label on the upper right that says C 117? The 7 is a European 7 with the vertical line straight and a crossbar. The 7 in the photos Dr. O'Shaughnessy showed us is an American 7 with the vertical line slanted and no crossbar. You've told me that forgers miss little details pretty often. Unless somebody replaced the old label with a new one, and I can't think of any honest reason why they'd do that, the plaque that Clarence Harshaw had might not be the same one Leonora Blake knew about."

He glanced at her, then at the photo, and got to his feet. "Thank you. You may just have kept the Heydonian from making a very serious mistake. If you'll excuse me for a moment—"

The door of his study closed behind him a moment later. Ariel watched it shut, then heard the faint muffled sounds of the beginning of a phone conversation. With a shrug, she got her cup of tea, slumped back onto the couch, and started reading the next chapter of the Raymond Chandler mystery.

She was only a few pages into the story when Dr. Moravec came back out of his study, looking a little less stressed. He settled in his chair, sipped at his tea, closed his eyes for a moment and then opened them again. "Your timing," he said, "was very good."

"I wish," said Ariel, looking at the floor. "I had a feeling when I first read *The Carnelian Moon* that I was missing something, and I couldn't figure out what it was. If I hadn't been as dumb as a brick we would have known about this days ago, and maybe things wouldn't have gone the way they did." Then, curiosity winning out: "So what happened?"

"The *Mercury* published an article this morning on the upcoming exhibit, and it had details on the exhibits that weren't supposed to be public yet. Somebody in the museum staff was talking considerably too freely."

"That's what Austin told me," Ariel said, and reddened when she realized she'd used his first name.

A quick wry glance from her grandfather told her he hadn't missed the reference. "The trustees are going to make some inquiries, and disciplinary action will probably be involved. The point that matters just now is that the article discussed the plaque in enough detail for it to be identified. So today a little after noon a gentleman named Istvan Horthy showed up at the Heydonian office: Hungarian by nationality, a private investigator by trade. He has a very specific line of work. He investigates art thefts and art forgeries."

She took that in. "And he knows about the plaque."

"He was in this country because of it."

"So is it stolen or forged?"

Dr. Moravec sipped at his tea, then said, "Both."

Ariel blinked in surprise, then laughed. "Okay. That's a story I want to hear."

"You're studying with Clarice Jackson tomorrow, as I recall. Can you be back here by five in the afternoon?" She nodded and he went on: "In that case you'll hear it from Mr. Horthy himself. I've invited him and several other people involved in this business to come here late tomorrow afternoon. Plenty of reputations are facing a certain amount of bruising over this business—the Harshaw estate, the antiquities dealer who appraised the plaque, certain members of the museum staff, and Dr. O'Shaughnessy, just to begin with. For that matter, it's quite possible that Gerard Breyer is going to have some explaining to do to his fellow werewolves."

She winced, thinking of one werewolf in particular, and tried to hide the reaction behind her teacup. A glance at her grandfather showed how little that had accomplished. "I take it," he said, "that Austin Wronski meant something to you."

"He seemed really nice," said Ariel. "I liked talking with him. I thought I'd made a friend, and I was considering—" She stopped and gestured with her free hand, brushing aside her daydreams. "Well, it doesn't really matter now, does it? He was doing it to try to get information out of me. I don't think I fell for it." She looked down. "But, yeah, I kind of fell for him. And now I feel like the world's biggest idiot, partly because it didn't occur to me to be suspicious of him, and partly because I missed what Leonora Blake wrote about the plaque." She forced a smile onto her face. "I don't think I have any reputation at all yet, but if I did, I'd be one of the people with bruises on it."

"Maybe so," said Dr. Moravec. "But because you did eventually notice what Leonora wrote, I've been able to convince the board to take Horthy's claims seriously, and we should be able to wrap up this whole case by tomorrow."

"I hope so," Ariel said. "At this point I'm pretty sick of it."

CHAPTER 17

THE GODDESS OF THE WILD

Ariel got home from Aunt Clarice's shop the next day in plenty of time. She trotted up to her room, shed the comfortable jeans and tee shirt she'd worn for the day's work and put on a moss green skirt and a pale green blouse: thrift store finds, both of them, but elegant. A quick brushing reduced her hair to some semblance of order. She was just starting down the stair when Dr. Moravec got home, and not much past halfway down when she realized he wasn't alone.

"Good afternoon, my Jumbly Girl," said Theophilus Cray as she came into sight. He'd just shed his voluminous gray coat and hung it on the coat tree, and was setting a small package wrapped in brown paper just below the coat. "You'll be gracing this little soirée with your presence? Excellent. Most of the attendees don't know you, and so it's just possible that your presence will keep a fistfight from breaking out."

Ariel choked. Dr. Moravec, once he'd shed his coat, said, "I don't think there's any risk of that. Ariel, do you mind coping with the coffee? I expect five more people shortly."

"Sure," said Ariel, and turned to Cray. "Thank you for the copy of *The Carnelian Moon*." She forced a smile. "I don't know if my grandfather told you about the photo."

"Yes, he mentioned that," said Cray. "But I trust you also enjoyed the novel." Ariel nodded enthusiastically, and he went on: "I bought up the remaining stock of all her books when the publisher finally went bankrupt, so I could give copies to people who might appreciate them. I'm glad to hear that one of her strays found a good home." He nodded once, as though he'd proved a point, and went into the parlor.

By the time the coffee maker was clearing its throat loudly in the kitchen, the others had begun to arrive. Dr. O'Shaughnessy was the first in the door, but just after him came a middle-aged woman in a jacket, a knee-length skirt, and strawberry-blonde hair just touched with gray. Her face was set hard, her mouth a straight line under visible pressure. "Angela Pittsfield," Dr. Moravec said, introducing her. "Representing the creditors of the Harshaw estate." She took a seat, thawed slightly when Ariel brought her coffee.

The doorbell chimed again. Dr. Moravec answered it, and admitted two more guests. The first was a tall black man with gold-rimmed glasses and a precisely trimmed goatee. "Michael McCutcheon," said Dr. Moravec, "representing the Harshaw estate." The second, to Ariel's surprise, was Gerard Breyer. He nodded a guarded greeting to Ariel. Dr. Moravec introduced him to the others as a scholar specializing in the traditions surrounding the plaque, fielded a coolly amused glance from Breyer in response.

Ariel had just finished getting coffee for the newcomers when the doorbell sounded again. She set the coffee pot down and went to the door. The last guest, to her even greater surprise, was the bland, balding little man in the heavy black coat she'd seen earlier at the county courthouse and the Heydonian. He seemed just as startled to see her as she was to see him. A sudden guess leapt to her mind, but she set it aside for the moment and greeted him.

"Thank you," he said in response; his English had a slight accent. "I am Istvan Horthy. You, I believe, are Ariel Moravec? Very good." He took off his coat, hung it from the coat tree with the others, and followed her into the parlor.

Introductions and one more cup of coffee followed. Ariel settled into a chair—the sofa had been claimed by Breyer and Theophilus Cray—and waited for Horthy to speak.

"So," he said once the preliminaries were finished. "Thank you for meeting with me. I understand the informality of this event. What is said can be off the record if you prefer."

"It'll be public soon enough," said McCutcheon.

"No doubt. But how soon, and how it is presented—that is not my concern."

McCutcheon nodded. Horthy glanced at the others, and went on. "So. I believe you know that I am a private investigator specializing in the art trade. Six years ago I was retained by the heirs of a man named Samuel Roth—a most interesting man. He was born in the United States in 1924 but relocated to France in 1938; his father had died, you understand, and he and his mother went to live with her brother and his family in Lyon.

"Her brother, Jacques Hirschberg, was a dealer in antiquities, and his specialty was items related to ancient religion and magic. That made him twice a target once the Germans conquered France in 1940: because of his Jewish faith but also because the Nazi Party had an unwholesome interest in magical things. Since the family was in the south of France they were spared persecution early on, and thought they might escape it entirely—very unwise of them. But the antiquities, those they expected the Germans to seize, and they were quite correct. In the fall of 1941 certain officials of the SS arrived and took everything.

"As an antiquities dealer, Hirschberg was of course well aware of all the tricks used to pass replicas off as originals. He did not wish to have his favorite pieces taken by the Germans, and it so happened that his nephew was a very talented artist. So as soon as France fell, he and his sister and nephew set out to create the most perfect possible copies of the prizes of his collection, which the Germans could be allowed to find and steal, while the originals were buried two meters underground and a small orchard planted above them.

"So that is what happened. I am sorry to say that Samuel Roth was the only member of the family to survive the war, for the others in his family were rounded up by the Germans in 1943 and died, some at Dachau and some at Theresienstadt. Roth escaped and spent the rest of the war with the Resistance, working as a forger of documents, at which he became very skilled. After the war was over he stayed in Lyon for a time, then moved to Vienna in 1956, married, raised a family, and spent the rest of a very long life there. He apparently never spoke of his wartime experiences, and only after his death did his family find out about the Hirschberg forgeries and the three chests of antiquities buried in the back garden of a house in Lyon the family still happened to own."

"Why did he keep it secret all that time?" Pittsfield asked. "That sounds suspicious."

"As it should, madam," said Horthy. "The reason, of course, is that he remained in the same trade. Nothing else he could do was as lucrative as forging antiquities, and he had a family to provide for. He did not want to do anything that would cast suspicion on his later forgeries, and admitting to that part of his wartime work would have done that all too well. Of course after he died that was not an issue, since his children were all established in their own professions and he had been a widower for nearly twenty years when his time finally came. So he left a sum of money in his will to pay for an investigator to track down those early pieces of his and inform their owners that, as you Americans say, they have been had.

"So that is the story of Samuel Roth. Its relevance here and now, of course, is that a certain bronze plaque with a carnelian inset, sold to an American collector by a Spanish antiquities dealer in 1949, is one of the pieces that Roth forged. The Spanish dealer turns out to have handled a large cache of items taken by the Ahnenerbe, the occult-research branch of the SS.

I am not sure how they obtained the cache, but obtain it they did, and invented false provenances for every item. What they did not know is that some of the stolen items they sold were no better than the provenances they invented. It is a fine irony, you must admit." He rubbed his hands together. "I knew that the bronze plaque had been sold to a collector here. I had identified its previous owner when an article in your local paper told me its present whereabouts—and here we are."

A dead silence followed his last word. Angela Pittsfield broke it. "I trust you're prepared to give some evidence for these claims of yours."

"Of course," Horthy said. "My office in Budapest is prepared to send an extensive dossier on this or any other piece of Roth's on request. Perhaps I may have your business card." She gave him an edged look, but handed it over.

Another silence passed. Ariel glanced around the gathering to make sure no one else was about to speak, and said, "May I ask a question?"

"Of course," said Horthy.

"The paper label on the back of the plaque," she ventured, "the one that reads C 117. The number 7 on the copy is different from the one on the original. Do you know why?"

Horthy turned toward her with a broad smile. His eyes, Ariel noticed with a start, didn't point the same direction. "Excellent! You noticed that. Roth was raised in America, as I said, and he wrote numbers in the American way. He was still a little incautious in those days, though he learned better later on. It is a clue that has helped me several times already. But I must ask how you knew about the original."

For answer she got up and crossed the parlor to the end table beside the sofa. A quick motion opened *The Carnelian Moon* to the photo. She handed the book to him, and he examined it, flipped forward to the title page, turned back to the photo. "Very clever of you. I was not aware of the existence of this photograph."

"May I see it?" Pittsfield asked.

Ariel took it to her. The book went from hand to hand, and finally returned to Ariel.

"Please come to my office tomorrow," said Pittsfield to Horthy. Her face was even more taut than before. "We'll need an affidavit from you, as well as the dossier you mentioned."

"Of course," said Horthy.

She stood up. "In that case, I think my business here is finished." To McCutcheon: "Please have it sold for anything it will bring." McCutcheon sent a bland uncommunicative smile her way, and she turned and went to the entry without another word. Dr. Moravec rose and followed her, let her out, and returned.

"We'll have to have the plaque reappraised," said McCutcheon then, still smiling. "I wonder if you have any idea what Roth's other items have sold for."

"Very little," said Horthy. "A few of the larger pieces have been placed with Jewish museums and Holocaust memorials, because of their history, you understand. But there are more than sixty such pieces, and the plaque is small and not especially striking. It might bring a few hundred dollars at most, if you can find a buyer."

Ariel waited a moment and then said, "I know someone who might want it." When McCutcheon turned to her: "Holly Harshaw, Clarence Harshaw's sister. When I interviewed her she mentioned that she liked it."

"I'll certainly ask her," said McCutcheon. "Thank you." He put a note on his phone, said his goodbyes and left. "So," said Horthy once he was gone. "Anything else I can clarify?"

"I have a question," said Breyer. "The originals, the ones you said were buried under an orchard. Have those been recovered?"

"Of course. They are in Vienna now, in the hands of the family, but there is talk of an exhibition in Lyon and another in Florence." Breyer smiled in response, a wolf's smile.

"Anything else?" said Horthy. There was nothing, and so he thanked them and went to the door, accompanied by Dr. Moravec.

In his absence Dr. O'Shaughnessy turned to look at Breyer. He said nothing, but after a moment Breyer turned the same edged smile in his direction. "Austin and I made an agreement," Breyer said, "and we'll keep it. It doesn't bind anyone else."

"You could buy the plaque," Dr. O'Shaughnessy said, his voice flat.

"No." Breyer's nose wrinkled as though he smelled something bad. "Paying money for it would be an affront to the god. It must be taken."

Dr. O'Shaughnessy considered him. "I'll make a few phone calls."

"By all means do so." Breyer smiled at him again, then stood as Dr. Moravec came back into the parlor. "Well, my dear doctor, it seems that you and your granddaughter saved Austin and me from making a very awkward mistake. You have my gratitude." He turned a less edged smile on the others present. "A good evening to you all. Perhaps I'll see you some other time."

Once he was gone and Dr. Moravec had settled in his chair, Dr. O'Shaughnessy allowed a harsh laugh. "Cold-blooded, that one. Interesting that he didn't ask about this." He reached into his pocket and put a familiar shape of patina-covered metal on the coffee table.

"The replica?" Dr. Moravec asked.

"It's a nice piece of work for a forgery." Dr. O'Shaughnessy sat back. "Do you want it? The sooner it's out of the Heydonian the less likely we are to get awkward questions."

No one spoke. Ariel considered it, the wolves and the great crimson moon, and to her own surprise found herself asking, "May I have it?"

A quick glance passed between the two doctors. Then Dr. O'Shaughnessy said, "You may indeed. Worth not much more than you'll pay for it, but it's not bad as a keepsake." She blushed and thanked him, and he got up. "Well. Now that that's settled, I'd better soothe some ruffled feathers back at the old pile."

The door opened and closed, Dr. Moravec came back to the parlor yet again, and then there were just the three of them: Ariel, Dr. Moravec, and Theophilus Cray, who hadn't said anything but the emptiest of pleasantries the whole time. "Thank you, Bernard," he said once Dr. Moravec settled back in his chair. "You were quite right, of course: Gerard Breyer is worth close study. Did you notice that he shaves between his eyebrows?"

Ariel gave him a startled look. "How can you tell?"

"Look closely and you'll see stubble, not the little colorless hairs on skin that don't need to be shaved. Oh, and he uses an electric razor. Nothing else roughens the skin like that." Cray sat back. "I wonder if you noticed anything in particular about Istvan Horthy."

"I'm pretty sure he's the one who followed me the day of our lesson, and the time before then," said Ariel. "I saw him both days, at the courthouse and the Heydonian."

"Good," said Cray. "Very good. Yes, our snark may well have been a boojum; it's quite possible that you're correct." To Dr. Moravec: "You have his contact information, I trust? Excellent. I'll give him a call in the next day or so. I have several questions to ask him, and I'll add that to the list. Oh, and before I forget."

He got to his feet, quick as a jack-in-the-box, and went out to the entry. In his absence Dr. Moravec considered Ariel, and Ariel looked at the floor.

Cray came back promptly with the parcel wrapped in brown paper. "Here you are, my Jumbly Girl. This is for you: even more appropriate than I thought, given today's other addition to your art collection." His gesture indicated the replica plaque on the table. He handed her the parcel. A foot tall and less than half that wide or deep, it was heavier than she expected.

She set it down on the coffee table and started pulling off the wrappings. The brown paper gave way to a wrapping of heavy green silk, hemmed at the edges and faded with age. That gave way in turn to a slender statue of white marble, maybe eight inches high, fashioned in a slightly gawky imitation of the ancient Greek style: a young woman in a sleeveless knee-length tunic and sandals, her weight shifting forward onto one leg, her head turned, one hand raised as though in blessing, the other reaching down to rest on the head of some unseen creature. The statue had led a rough life, that was clear from cracks and surface damage, but it was still intact.

Enchanted, Ariel let out a little low cry. "Yes, I thought you would appreciate it," said Cray. "It belonged to Aunt Leonora. It's a late Roman copy of a much older original, and not in pristine condition by any means, but this is the goddess Feronia, the sister of Soranus. She was the Faliscan goddess of wild places, their equivalent of Artemis and Diana. A fitting gift for a young lady of antique tastes, I believe."

Ariel stammered out her thanks, and Cray beamed in response. "You're most welcome, my Jumbly Girl. I'm in a fine mood tonight. I learned earlier that the Harshaw estate accepted my bids for a good many items: everything that would have gone to me, or to other members of my family, if Jasper Harshaw hadn't been better financed than I was. So quite a few people I know, or their children, will have the things they should have gotten all those years ago." He turned to Dr. Moravec. "You're sure—"

"Thank you, but yes." Dr. Moravec's face was even more impassive than usual.

Ariel glanced from her grandfather to Cray and back, uncertain. "Theophilus," said Dr. Moravec, "offered me my choice of mementoes from Leonora's collection. A generous offer, but—" He gestured, dismissing it. "At this point in my life I have more mementoes than I know what to do with, and a gift from Leonora already." In response to Ariel's questioning glance, he motioned with his chin to where the little wooden crocodile grinned down at them.

"That was hers," said Ariel.

"One of two," Cray said, with a smile unnervingly like the crocodile's. "The other haunts a similar spot in my library." He considered her, then went on: "But I hope I can ask the two of you to have dinner with me tonight. I am quite absurdly happy, you see, and misery may love company but happiness has an even more serious case of the same habit."

They agreed, and Ariel set the marble statue down on its side on the coffee table for safety's sake. Cray beamed at her. Then: "Ah, but I'm getting forgetful, aren't I? The thing I trust you noticed about Istvan Horthy. Did you observe his eyes?"

Ariel paused, then said, "Yes. Yes, I did. They didn't point the same way. I don't know what that means, though."

"Excellent. You noticed, and you recognized the limits of your knowledge. What that means, my Jumbly Girl, is that he only has one eye. The other is glass."

Ariel remembered the warning she'd gotten from Aunt Clarice, and flinched. By then Cray had turned toward the door, and didn't seem to notice.

The rest of the evening was pleasant enough, and the next morning at Aunt Clarice's began propitiously with a lesson on brewing Van Van oil. "Lots of folks do this the cheap way," Aunt Clarice told her two pupils, "and just throw in some scent oils." She allowed herself the luxury of a disdainful sniff. "Do that and it won't have half the power it has if you do it right."

Ariel wasn't minded to argue. Doing it right, though, turned out to involve heating a big kettle mostly full of vegetable oil on a portable burner in the back room, waiting until the oil was just short of simmering, and then keeping it at that temperature while adding carefully chosen herbs by the handful and stirring with a big wooden spoon. Once the oil was ready, a condition Aunt Clarice judged by watching the way bits of floating herb sizzled at the edges, the kettle had to be lifted off the burner without spilling and set on a cooling rack, then stirred again at intervals while Aunt Clarice passed on some of the dozens of ways that Van Van oil could be used in magic, speaking fast enough that Ariel had to push her shorthand skills to their limits to get everything down.

By the time the oil had been strained and set to cool in a second kettle, the reek of hot oil, vervain, and lemon grass in the back room was overpowering. Opening the windows onto the alley let in cold raw air laced with car exhaust but didn't clear the smell noticeably. It didn't help that once the oil was cooling, Aunt Clarice brought in a five pound package of valerian root she'd received the day before from some herbal supply house on the other side of the country, and left Ariel and Cassie to divide it up into packets for sale while she did tea leaf readings for clients. To Ariel, valerian root smelled more or less like dirty sweatsocks. Once its scent blended with the other smells in the room, Ariel ended up wishing she owned a gas mask.

Still, she had something she needed to do. She waited until Aunt Clarice was gone and she and Cassie had talked about three or four things that didn't matter. That was when she asked, "Got any plans for this coming Saturday?"

"Not yet," said Cassie. "Why?"

"You heard about the new exhibit at the Heydonian, right? That's opening day and there's a reception. I've got an invite and a guest pass, if you're interested."

She'd expected—what? Maybe a yes, maybe a no, maybe some questions, but certainly not a long silent considering look she couldn't read at all. "What is it?" she asked.

"Not everybody wants to be seen in that kind of place with a Southie girl," Cassie said.

"I'm not everybody," Ariel snapped back, meeting her gaze squarely.

Another silence went by. Then Cassie let a little smile slip out. "Okay," she said. "Yeah, I want to see the exhibit and a reception would be fun, so yes, please." Then, tilting her head to one side: "What are you going to wear?"

"You remember the little black thing Audrey Hepburn wore in *Breakfast at Tiffany's*?" Cassie nodded, and Ariel went on. "I found one just like it at a thrift store a couple of months ago. I got a little black purse with spaghetti straps to go with it, too."

That earned her a sudden luminous grin. "Okay," Cassie said. "If you're going in a thrift store dress I'm not going to worry about a thing."

"Good." Ariel considered her for a moment, gathered up her courage and said, "Can I ask a favor? I had a pretty lousy childhood but I know I had a lot of stuff you didn't. If I ever say something really stupid because of that, could you kick me or something and shut me up?"

"Nope," said Cassie. "I'd rather you say something than clam up the way you do."

Ariel gave her an uneasy look. Cassie met it with a bland smile. "Okay," said Ariel. "Is it going to be any kind of trouble for you to get a nice dress?"

Cassie shook her head. "Nope," she said again. "Mom's really good at sewing. You have to sew if you're a mudang, stores don't sell the clothes you need, but my grandma says she's better than anyone else in the family. I bet I can come up with something."

CHAPTER *18*

THE AUTUMN MOON IS BRIGHT

She did, too. When Saturday afternoon came around at last, the doorbell rang at the time they'd agreed upon. Ariel opened the door to find Cassie standing there in a knee-length silk dress the color of jade, her hair tied back with a ribbon of the same fabric. "Wow," Ariel said, motioning her in. "Your mom made that? It's gorgeous."

"Says Miss Holly Golightly," Cassie said, grinning. "That's one classy dress. And the pearls, too—really nice."

Ariel blushed; she'd spent most of an hour fussing over her outfit and getting her hair to behave. She gestured at her friend. "Show me."

Cassie pirouetted slowly. The ribbon holding her hair was tied in an ornate knot that looked like a butterfly. When she finished turning, she glanced past Ariel, and panic showed briefly in her expression before she forced a smile in its place. Ariel didn't have to hear quiet footfalls on the floorboards to guess why, and stepped out of the way.

"Ms. Jackson," Dr. Moravec said, and pressed her hand. He was in a black suit a little more neatly tailored than usual, and had a curious seven-sided gold symbol fixed to his lapel. "A pleasure to meet you. I know your father, of course, and Ariel's spoken of you." He motioned toward the door. "Shall we?"

They went down the sidewalk to the old black Buick. Dr. Moravec held the back door for them and then got behind the wheel. As they pulled away from the curb, Ariel sent a questioning glance Cassie's way. Cassie replied with a grin.

The on-street parking near the Heydonian had filled up by the time they got there, and the Buick had to settle for a spot most of three blocks away. Fortunately the day was clear and not too cold. By the time they got within sight of the Heydonian's entrance, half a dozen other people were headed the same direction. The great bronze door swung open, the entrance hall welcomed them with its usual austere hush, and their footfalls joined with others to set echoes scurrying in the coffered ceiling high above.

The doors of the museum stood open, but a discreet sign standing nearby said CLOSED FOR PRIVATE EVENT. A lean usher with graying hair and the face of an irritable vulture stood guard with a tablet in his hand, checking in the guests: a longtime employee, Ariel guessed, for he recognized certain people by sight and motioned them in without a word, while asking others for their names. It didn't surprise Ariel at all to be asked. She made herself smile, handed him the two passes, and said, "Ariel Moravec and guest." The man nodded as though it was the most obvious thing in the world, and motioned them through.

The lobby space inside was bustling with people. Ariel's memories of the same space—the shadow-ridden emptiness the morning after she'd chased werewolves through Adocentyn's streets—clashed with present reality: a bright busy space with high ceilings, full of talkative people in various modes of formal dress, from old men in black suits with white ties to young women whose dresses went through the motions of pretending to be daring. Some of them, she guessed, were shareholders, some trustees, some donors, some family members of one or another category or guests that they'd invited, and nearly all of them were utterly unknown to her.

Before she could finish glancing around, someone extracted himself from a conversation and came toward her grandfather: a man in late middle years, very obese, with a gray silk waistcoat stretched over a capacious belly, black coat and trousers, and a pearl-gray ascot tied loosely at his throat. His face was as pink as a baby's but creased with an edged wariness no baby could have imitated. His hair, gray touched with black, was combed straight back over the top of his head. "Moravec?" he said, in a light tenor voice. "There you are."

"Good afternoon, Domitian," said Dr. Moravec blandly. "I don't believe you've met my granddaughter or her friend. Ariel Moravec, Cassiopeia Jackson, this is Domitian Lorber."

"Pleased to meet you," Ariel said.

Lorber's massive hand closed over hers with a delicacy that startled her, released it. He did the same with Cassie's, then gave them both a crisp nod of dismissal and turned to Dr. Moravec. "I trust you can spare a moment. I have some news you'll need to hear."

Dr. Moravec said something equally bland and let Lorber lead him away to one side of the crowd, where a little knot of elderly people gathered. No surprises there, Ariel thought, and let herself drift along with Cassie in the crowd.

A moment or so after that an old woman in black with a face as pale as a ghost's glanced Ariel's way, nodded a greeting, and turned back to a conversation. Ariel had to wrestle with her memories for a moment before recognizing her: Margaret Hynd, the minister at St. Cyprian's church in downtown Adocentyn. Moments later a more familiar face approached Ariel.

"Why, my Jumbly Girl!" said Theophilus Cray. "A pleasure to see you here." He was wearing another of his unfashionable suits, this one dove-gray with narrow lapels, and a little flat cap of red silk brocade on his head that failed to do much to corral his flyaway hair. She said something suitable, and he went on: "Perhaps you can introduce me to your friend."

"Of course. Cassiopeia Jackson, Theophilus Cray."

He pressed Cassie's hand, and then startled Ariel by speaking to Cassie in a language Ariel barely recognized as Korean. Cassie looked just as startled, but replied in the same language, and they talked for a few minutes. Then Cray extracted a business card and handed it to Cassie, and Cassie got a card of her own and a pen out of her purse, wrote something on the back in what Ariel guessed was Korean, and handed the card to Cray. He bowed to her in the Asian manner, she bowed in reply, he beamed at them both, and away he went, looking pleased with himself.

"What did Mr. Cray say to you?" said Ariel. "If it's okay to ask."

"He knew I'm a mudang in training," Cassie said, looking startled. "Just by looking at me. I was sure your grandpa or someone must have told him, but he said no. He wants Mom to do some ceremonies for him."

"He spent a long time in Siberia with shamans," said Ariel.

"Okay, that would explain it. I'll let Mom know."

Minutes passed. The chairman of the board of trustees, a frail old woman in a frilly yellow dress, went to a podium over on one side of the lobby, got everyone's attention, said a few words, announced that the exhibit was open, and then settled into a nearby chair as though the effort had exhausted her. The attendees began filing into the exhibit space, and Ariel and Cassie let themselves be drawn along.

They were through the first room and had started into the second when a face Ariel recognized emerged from the crowd and made a beeline toward her. "Ms. Moravec," said Holly Harshaw, looking uncomfortable. "I wonder if I could talk to you for a moment."

A quick glance at Cassie got a smile and a shooing motion. Ariel followed Harshaw over to one corner of the room, where a glass case held pottery jars covered with incantations to make them traps for evil spirits. "I—I wanted to thank you," said the older woman. "The people with my brother's estate told me you said they should offer me the plaque with the wolves."

"Did you get it?" Ariel asked, and when Harshaw nodded: "Okay, good. I'm glad."

That earned her an uncertain look. "You meant what you said."

"About having stuff taken away that I cared about? Yeah."

"Well, thank you." She glanced back the way they'd come, got an even more uncertain look on her face, and went a different direction. When Ariel copied the glance, she spotted Cassie and Kyle Harshaw talking, and went toward them as casually as she could.

"That's vitiligo, right?" Cassie asked. Kyle said something inaudible, and she went on: "One of my cousins has it bad. I bet you got a lot of crap for it in school."

"Way too often," said Kyle. "They called me Appaloosa Archie, after the Pony Pal."

"Jerks," Cassie said in a fine tone of scorn.

The look he sent Cassie's way in response made Ariel veer in another direction, into the next room, where the corroded green mass of the Kynokefale machine and the gleaming bronze replica were the center of attention. Ariel decided to wait until the crowd had thinned, and went instead to a display of cracked tortoise shells with obscure characters scratched into them: a divination method from ancient China, the placard on the wall said.

She was trying to guess what the characters and the cracks had to do with one another when someone else came to look at the same exhibit. She glanced toward him after a moment. It was Istvan Horthy, and he was considering her with a smile.

"Ms. Moravec," he said. "A pleasure to meet you again. Especially so, because I gather from Mr. Cray that I caused you a certain degree of alarm two weeks ago."

"So you were the one who was following me," she ventured.

"I was indeed. I was in search of the whereabouts of the plaque, as you know, and had the name of Leonora Blake as its purchaser. I needed a copy of her will, and the clerk mentioned that the young woman who left as I was entering the office had just obtained the same will. So my suspicions were roused, as you might say. I found out what else you had learned, and was waiting when you left the estate sales office. Then—" He smiled and shrugged. "You escaped me rather neatly by boarding the bus. Very clever of you.

"Then I encountered you again a few days later here at the Heydonian. I was certain then that you were after the same thing I was, but when I followed you, I found someone else following me. An enticing puzzle! But I succeeded in learning your name and discovering that you work for Dr. Moravec, so I was no longer worried that you might be, for example, with a ring of art thieves. But I apologize if I caused you any worry."

"It's okay," said Ariel. "Seriously."

"I am glad to hear it." Then, considering her again. "I hope you will keep at the investigator's trade. You made me work to keep you in sight, and not everyone can say that." Flustered, she thanked him, and he smiled and headed off into the crowd.

She'd just managed to spend some time looking at the Kynokefale machine when Cassie rejoined her. "Well, that was interesting."

"Kyle Harshaw?" When she nodded: "Did you give him your phone number?"

"Yeah. He seems pretty nice." A shrug dismissed him. "We'll see."

They went through the rest of the museum more or less in each other's company. There was plenty to see, all of it interesting, and well before they reached the last of the rooms Ariel was feeling more than a little overwhelmed by the sheer richness of the ancient world's magic.

The sequence of rooms finally brought them back around to the lobby, where they found Dr. Moravec over near one wall, in the middle of an earnest conversation with Theophilus Cray and an old woman Ariel didn't know: tall, stocky and thick-legged, her white hair in a braid that went most of the way down her back, wearing a dark blue dress that was almost aggressive in its dowdiness. Cassie gave Ariel an uncertain glance, and Ariel herself tried to guess whether she should approach or stay back. Fortunately Cray spotted them and said, "And here they are. Ms. Moravec, Ms. Jackson, perhaps I can introduce you to Ms. Branwen Falkenberg. Branwen? Bernard's granddaughter Ariel, and her friend Cassiopeia, one of Clarice Jackson's great-nieces."

"Pleased to meet you," said Ms. Falkenberg. Her voice was deep, with a noticeable German accent. She put out a hand, which both the girls pressed.

"Now that we've all been introduced," Cray went on, "may I invite the two of you to join the three of us for dinner, my treat?" Ariel agreed at once, but Cassie said, "I'll have to check with my folks." With a little smile: "They might have something planned."

"Good," Ms. Falkenberg said. "Your parents taught you well. Your father is maybe Leo Jackson? Tell him I will be there."

Cassie blinked, but managed another smile and said, "I'll do that." She wove her way through a scattering of people to a different wall, where she got out her cell phone. She was back a minute or two later and said to Cray, "Thank you and I'd be delighted." Cray beamed.

"Did you tell him?" Ms. Falkenberg asked.

"Yes, I did. He knows you, doesn't he?"

"He arrested me twice." A gesture dismissed the matter. "All in the past." She turned to Cray. "Theophilus, perhaps you will drive me; it is that or a taxi. Shall we?"

A few minutes later Ariel, Cassie, and Dr. Moravec were on the sidewalk outside the Heydonian, on their way back to the Buick. The sky was full of stars, and the moon had just begun to rise, splashing pale light over the eastward sides of buildings.

The autumn moon is bright, Ariel thought, remembering the phrase, and winced inwardly.

"Is it okay if I ask about Ms. Falkenberg?" Cassie asked Dr. Moravec.

"Of course." They reached the car, he unlocked it, and held the door. Once they were all inside and the engine was grumbling irritably to itself, he went on. "Branwen's a remarkable person. Welsh mother, Austrian father, as the name suggests. She's in the same trade as your mother: a medium, a very good one. I've consulted with her spirit guide more than once to settle some detail of an investigation."

Cassie nodded as though that was the most obvious thing in the world. "I think the Reverend Mother at church does consultations like that sometimes."

"Matilda Tepper?" Cassie beamed and nodded. "Yes, I've discussed cases with her a few times as well. Another very capable practitioner."

The Buick pulled away from the curb, found its way out of downtown through light traffic and went north, through neighborhoods Ariel didn't know. A mile or so from the Heydonian, Dr. Moravec guided the car into a narrow parking lot next to a one-story brick building with plate glass windows spilling light out onto the street. The sign above the door read CHEZ PÉLADAN, which cheered Ariel—she'd glanced into a book by a mage of that name, and liked what she'd read of it.

Inside the air was full of conversation in more than one language, shimmering instrumental music from loudspeakers overhead, scents from bouquets of roses at every table contending with the scents of food and wine and somehow coming out ahead. Cray and Branwen Falkenberg had gotten there already and staked out a table for five in a convenient corner. The greeter, a plump bustling man with a pencil-thin mustache, led the way there, got menus into everyone's hands, and hurried off.

The food was unfamiliar, at least to Ariel, but very good; the conversation ranged far and wide, and more than once Ariel ended up laughing herself into hiccups, when Cray uttered some drollery or Branwen Falkenberg said some absurdity with utter seriousness, only a little twist of one side of her mouth letting the others know she didn't mean it.

By the time they'd finished, that end of Adocentyn was sinking deeper into the hush of night. The moon streamed down as they retraced their steps to the Buick. "Thank you," Cassie said. "Both of you. This has been one wonderful day and evening."

"I'm delighted to hear that," said Dr. Moravec. Ariel managed to say something more or less appropriate. The moonlight pushed her thoughts in directions she desperately didn't want them to go, but she was too tired to start a conversation.

The streets were empty enough that it didn't take long to reach Cassie's house and drop her off. Once she'd thanked them again, waved, and gone inside her house, Ariel moved to the passenger seat, slumped back into it, and said, "Well, that's over with." Then, catching herself: "The case, I mean."

Dr. Moravec's glance communicated nothing. "In a manner of speaking," he said. "When Domitian Lorber pulled me aside just after we arrived, he had news from Austria. There was a competent and daring daylight robbery in a house in the Mariahilf district of Vienna owned by one Josef Roth. No suspects, only one thing stolen. I'm sure I don't have to tell you what it was."

"So the werewolves got it," said Ariel.

"Almost certainly, yes." He pulled away from the curb. "And of course Breyer and his apprentice are still in town. I'll be surprised if we don't hear about them again at some point."

Ariel winced and dropped the subject. Another minute or two brought the old car to rest beside the curb not far from the house on Lyon Avenue. As they got inside, Ariel remembered the one remaining thing she'd meant to ask. "So tell me about Domitian Lorber."

That earned her an amused glance. "I'd be interested in hearing first about what you thought of him."

"I don't trust him," said Ariel. "I don't know why, but I don't trust him."

"Wise of you." Dr. Moravec pulled off his coat, hung it from the coat tree. "Lorber's a member of the Heydonian's board of trustees. In a certain sense he's a rival of mine, though we have more in common than not: neither of us are from Adocentyn originally, for example. Lorber's very wealthy, he's an extremely competent mage, and he has all the ethics of a shark in the middle of a feeding frenzy." With a fractional shrug: "With any luck you'll never have to deal with him outside of social occasions."

A few more words settled the remaining details of the night, and she climbed the familiar stair, telling herself that she'd had a wonderful time. That would have been the truth, too, except that every step of the way she'd sensed the shadow of the afternoon and evening she'd hoped to have, the first date with Austin, maybe the beginning of something that might have mattered.

She got to her room, closed the door, shed her jewelry and clothes, pulled on a baggy sleep shirt and an old plaid bathrobe against the chill. Dress, shoes, purse, pearls went to out-of-the-way places behind more practical things. All the while, the shadow remained. So did the room's newest occupant, the little statue of the goddess Feronia. She stood in solitary state atop the bookcase with the green silk beneath her as a sort of altar cloth. The replica plaque with the carnelian moon stood above and behind her on the wall, held there by little brackets, creating a little shrine of sorts.

Ariel had spent hours deciding exactly where to put the statue. That mattered, though she could not have said why. Maybe, she told herself, it was because people a long time ago thought the statue was sacred, an image of something that soared high above the human; maybe it was because Leonora

Blake had loved the little statue; maybe it was something else. Now and again Ariel wondered whether there should be other items close by the statue, though she wasn't sure what those would be. Half-formed thoughts stirred in her when she looked at it, murmurs of an uncertain reverence she couldn't name and didn't yet know how to express.

She finished getting her clothes put away, stood there in the middle of the bedroom for a little while, irresolute. The shadow of the day that might have been still loomed over her. She considered throwing herself face first onto the bed and crying into her pillow, but there were no tears in her, just a bleak gray empty place where tears should have been.

You could go talk to him, her thoughts whispered to her. You could try.

She rolled her eyes, told herself that it was the last thing on earth she wanted to do. Then, with a little tired sigh, she went to her desk and got out her shewstone. The little origami crow, a gleam of blue, sat behind it. She made herself ignore it, sat down to begin her evening practice.

No wolf appeared in the crystal that night, or for many nights to come.

www.ingramcontent.com/pod-product-compliance
Lightning Source LLC
LaVergne TN
LVHW030848230625
814427LV00001B/41